FREEDOM RIDE

SHORT STORIES
AND POEMS

by

RON S. NOLAN

PLANETROPOLIS PUBLISHING

222 Santa Cruz Avenue, No. 11
Aptos, California 95003
www.planetropolis.com

This book is an original publication of
Planetropolis Publishing.

ISBN-10: 0578933527
ISBN-13: 978-0-578-93352-8

Special thanks to
Julie Kay Adams
for her love and support.

Metamorphosis Chronicles (Met Chron)™ explores the future of a human society that is confronted with the threats posed by rampant climate change and AI androids and robots that are competing with *Sapients* and *New-Humans* for jobs and natural resources on an over-populated planet Earth controlled by profit-driven, corporate governments.

Planetropolis Publishing
www.planetropolis.com

Dedicated to the Memory of
Michael H.D. Dormer

Mike Dormer was a close friend and an outstanding artist who is well known for developing the Hot Curl cartoon franchise of products based upon a 400 pound, iconic statue located at Windandsea Beach in Ocean Beach, California.

Mike, whom I called 'Mom' (due to all the advice and guidance that he gave me) was the best man at my last wedding. Before that Mike and I enjoyed many months together when he spent a hot summer at my beach house on the Big Island in Hawaii.

Mike was a master of the creative process and the art of thinking outside the box. This book is devoted to his memory. The cover painting was made especially for the Freedom Ride story—which after all these years is finally published. Thank you Mom!

TABLE OF CONTENTS

— *Freedom Ride* —

Planet Nuptia

R odano Orthrup, a muscular, copper-skinned, six foot tall human looking male, was born as an adopted only child and raised in Housing Unit 36 in Grid 333 on Planet Nuptia in the Andromeda Galaxy. He spent his youth attending the same classes as his fellow students, however he nearly always beat them at cognitive tests and physical exercise—which caught the attention of the '*Centurians*' that were capable of monitoring the position as well as every word spoken through the GPS and audio/video surveillance system which each citizen was required to have implanted into their foreheads at the age of five—except for select individuals that were designated as exempt by the *Centurian Masters*.

Watching and betting on broadcast sports was the most popular entertainment venue and for Rodano, surfing was an exciting, highly rewarding career. It was also an extremely dangerous sport.

After ten years of entering and winning contests, Rodano was exhausted and coming to the realization that soon he would join several of his colleagues and competitors that had recently retired from the sport due to concerns about the rising levels of toxic copper, iron and magnesium levels that were rapidly increasing in the ocean due to inland mining and the transport of hazardous materials from the frigid mountain poles to the tropical seas by three major rivers systems.

For Rodano, the final blow to his surfing career took place when two surfer pals, one male and one female, had been electrocuted during the yearly world surfing contest using new high tech wet suits that connected to a buffer circuit in the latest generation of surfboards.

Shaken by the news, yet determined to add one last World Surfer Champion trophy to his collection, Rodano scored the highest, won the lucrative winning prize and then, surprisingly to his corporate sponsors, announced his immediate retirement.

So...at last, Rodano entered college where he developed a keen understanding of the laws of physics and then went on to graduate school where he specialized in astrophysics. His Ph.D. dissertation hypothesized that Alfvén waves were generating magnetic fields of accelerating electrons that created the atmospheric auroras that frequently illuminated the horizon of the night sky and made the oceans glow at night. However, due to a lack of confirming data, his research had yet to receive any recognition.

That was about to change...

The experimental wave riding machine that Rodano had designed and was currently testing as part of his newly funded research at the PsiTech University, where he had recently been admitted as a new faculty member, was Rodano's strategy to acquire the 'hard data' needed to test his hypothesis that Alfvén waves were involved.

However, his academic position was seriously threatened by a recent citation that he received for not wearing his GPS tracker and surveillance system implant on three occasions in the last three months. His lawyer pal from college tried to claim that the implant was a threat to Rodano's health and safety due to his research which involved high voltage electronic systems.

But, the judge didn't buy it and stated. "Our Nuptian Society is based upon the ability to continuously monitor each individual's present location and observe what they say and do as they interact with their fellow citizens. Everyone must obey every instance of the law. Anyone that thinks that he or she is an independent soul will spend as much time in jail as needed until they learn their lesson. I mean how hard can it be?"

The judge pointed a vidcam at his forehead, then continued. "All you have to do is insert the *com tracker* into the cavity in the middle of your forehead. Look, see I am wearing mine. Do you see it Rodano?"

"Yes, I do, Sir!"

"OK. You are hereby sentenced to one month in jail. You must report tomorrow before noon or I will increase your sentence to ninety days. Do you hear me Rodano? I am giving you time in the morning to put your affairs in order, but I want you here by twelve noon tomorrow!"

"Yes, your Honor."

9 AM
Next Day

Back in his office, Rodano's mind was stirring with anticipation and resignation that this might be the most important day in his life and the fear that it could be his last. As he was checking his simulation model, he looked out the window and noticed that the sky was darkening right on schedule and just as his simulation had predicted—an indication that an Alfvén wave aurora of immense strength was beginning.

Rodano's prediction that extremely high energy levels would result as a consequence of Planet Nuptia's three moons entering into a precise, inline alignment creating high-powered Alfvén waves. The usual vista of a golden sun shining over a bright blue sea would be transformed into a fiery, resonating disc that would illuminate a horizon of glowing red surf. As the Alfvén waves grew in strength, pushing and concentrating the electrons from the sun's surface to its surrounding corona, the sky would turn pitch black. In spite of the warnings that Rodano delivered at several seminars and cloud media interviews, none of his research associates believed that this scenario would happen—including the judge, but his calculations indicated that the ocean surf should easily surpass the largest on planet Nuptia in the past—including a devastating tsunami in 2169.

'Great!' he thought. *'The timing couldn't be worse! A once in a lifetime wave surfing opportunity that will likely cost me months if not years in the slammer if I don't comply with the judge's mandate. This is tearing my soul to shreds.'*

FREEDOM RIDE

Arraignment Day

After a sleepless night, Rodano went to his office and called his attorney, but was told that he was in a meeting with instructions not to be disturbed. Rodano glanced again at the wave projections then rammed his fist down hard against his desk, dug the GPS tracker and tiny video/audio system out of his forehead, threw it to the floor and smashed it with the heel of his boot.

He yelled, 'Listen up judge...I know you are listening. I'll see you in Hell if you don't leave me alone and let me do the job that I am being paid for.'

The sky had quickly shifted from the usual blue to solid black as sirens wailed and helicopters flew over the beach carrying news reporters and weather experts who were totally caught off guard and could offer no explanation for the dramatic events taking place—not only here, but on the entire side of the planet facing the lined up moons.

The smooth, phosphorescent red swell slowly ramped up in power as Rodano impatiently squatted on his lean haunches, careful to avoid the blobs that had washed onto the shore. He checked his wrist-chrono; it indicated that the largest waves would begin arriving in about seventeen nipets (Earth equivalent: twenty minutes). He activated the wave machine's computer which monitored and recorded a wide variety of data about the surfboard's performance and the surrounding environmental conditions which were synced to his wrist-com. Finally, he set his video camera to record and document the red glowing waves with bright white spray at the top that radiated in the coal black sky.

He thought *The game is on!* as he caressed the sleek rails of the graceful crystalline surfboard and then tucked the transparent, two kilogram board under his arm and sprinted down to the beach where he hurriedly sprayed an aerosol adhesive on his board, allowed a moment for the excess powder to sublimate, and then slid onto his board in the swaying beach break.

Kneeling upon board's smooth surface, he dug deeply, working his way out to where the oncoming wave trains seemed to levitate above the multi-hued, crimson horizon. He was glad to have the boost capability of his new board's mini-sized power generator in reserve—he figured that it might come in handy some day if he was ever caught inside a big set that he couldn't manage on his own—or just needed to recover and catch his breath.

As he paddled out to the lineup, where the first incoming waves were peeling off, he looked down and shuddered at the sight of corpulent sponges, red-mottled sting rays flying among the pink table corals and fleshy, mutated coacervates that swayed on a carpet of luminous bubbles streaming up and forming a thick mat of large reddish, brown blobs that littered the beach sand.

Rodano had heard reports from the local surfer community warning about the instantaneous conversion of flesh to painful energy when a person accidentally stepped on and ruptured one of the blobs. Although they normally preyed upon fleshy, slow swimming goose fish, Rodano surmised that they would not recognize the difference between him and a goose fish—or care much about anything at all. Looking through his board, he saw a school of fat sculpins searching for dinner while avoiding the blobs and sting rays. Suddenly, the fish predators darted into cracks and crevices. Rodano figured that this signified the approach of big surf and dug in deeper to get to the lineup.

A strong gust of hot dry wind nearly knocked Rodano off his board. His gaze darted from the reef below to the sea horizon where a train of immense, red peaks marched toward the Red Cliff Beach shoreline.

Rodano took a deep breath and let the first comber slide by underneath his board as it lifted him like he was soaring upwards in a twenty story office elevator and then plunging him down in free fall as the wave passed beneath.

He lined up for the next wave, feverishly stroked and slid down the lofty wave front. He carefully balanced on the auto-reflex V-Tail and cut back under the wave crest, waiting for the wave to feel the bottom of the reef and surge upward to form a giant wall.

Suddenly, the wave formed perfectly and his board accelerated hard to Rodano's joy, precipitously streaking across the face of the mountainous wave. Rodano leaned forward driving his left foot to the nose of the board which caused the man-machine to explode down the wave. A glistening, fine spray of deep red fluid enveloped him as he slid toward the abyss at the bottom of the wave. The perfectly concentric tube seemed to extend infinitely ahead, but started to constrict, causing his board to accelerate even more.

Rodano fell to his knees and extended his arms— touching both sides of the ruby red tube as it drew in upon itself, shrieking like the gale winds of a tornado. Adding to the cacophony of sounds was the roaring thunder of the old fashioned, diesel engine locomotive that daily brought tourists from the capital city to Red Cliff Beach. Although the locomotive appeared to be a relic from decades past, in fact it employed a high tech levitation system that was so strong that kids took turns wearing shoes with maglev soles that allowed them to float in the air and do somersaults when the train passed by the playground next to the track.

When the wave temporarily slowed as it crossed a deep trench created by an ancient lava flow, Rodano looked up and saw a police airship with red flashing lights dangling a basket carrying an armed trooper who broadcast in a shrill voice, "Attention Citizen Rodano Orthrup, you are in violation of your court order. You are ordered to peacefully surrender. Be aware that we are authorized to use force if you do not comply."

Being conceived and raised on this dreadful planet was the culmination of a chain of horrors—still Rodano's heart raced with the thrill of speed and the wild diffraction spectrum splaying colors as the mist of copper red fluid prismatically bent the light overhead and the massive wave once more began to accelerate

After all—no one has ridden waves of this magnitude before. This ride will become my life's signature. No one can ever take it away from me.

Rodano, aware of the terrific forces propelling him, carefully trimmed the board to maintain its precise attack within the final hollow pipe of the wave. The board tingled with vibrations and started to hum as it surged ahead.

Suddenly, he swerved the board hard to the right and then back to avoid a spurt of projectile trails—most likely tranquilizer rounds fired by the officer, but he couldn't be sure.

He screamed, *'"You've got to be kidding me, Judge. Think of the most profane word you know and shove it you know where."*

Rodano checked his wrist-chrono. He could see that six of the seven lights were blinking a bright red. It was time to bail out or suffer disintegration when the powerful racing mass of grace smashed devastatingly onto the cliffs that lined the beach. Waiting until the last possible nippet, Rodano leaned fiercely into the wave nearly separating his board from his grip. In an instant he punched through the backside of the wave into a morass of turbulent soup. The turbulence sucked him down to within millimeters of the lethal fire coral and swept him past sculpins with extended fins wedged into crevices in the reef.

He stroked hard for the surface and was suddenly enveloped by a spinning orb of crackling, electrically charged foam that swept him behind one of the trains carrying passengers fleeing out of danger in the unexpected darkness. Just as the wave ahead collapsed and he was about to smash into cliff wall, his vision blacked out and he lost consciousness.

June 11, 2036
Mystery Cave

Once again the research team had assembled in the makeshift lab in the cave to run a followup set of tests designed to focus on the sounds that Madeline seemed to hear around the same time twice a day and now tracked by a floating hologram that displayed the time and sound wave graphics next to the wall in the cavern rear.

Torch asked Madeline, "I'm glad we have you

grounded with a seatbelt. Are you feeling comfortable?"

Madeline held up a water bottle and said, "I'm set. No sounds yet...hold it...I am picking up something."

Blips began to appear on the audio display and steadily grew in amplitude, stronger and louder and suddenly the cavern started to vibrate and lights on the mysterious racks of electronic equipment that lined the walls of the room flashed on and off, emitting chirps and beeps.

Madeline cried out. "That sounds like the train that Mom and I have been hearing for many years...even decades!"

Moments later, the group jumped back as a three meter circular window sprang open in the rear wall of the cave through which they stared in shock at the old fashioned locomotive towing what looked like several passenger cars that went steaming past and repeatedly blasting its whistle.

After the roar faded and the train vanished into the distance, they found a tall copper-hued male stranger lying on his back next to the window who appeared to be dazed, but otherwise uninjured.

Torch said, "Heh guys. Now we seem to have a visitor unless somehow he sneaked in here with us."

Chron asked, "I haven't seen him before. Anybody else recognize him?"

At first no one answered, then Astra replied, "He seems human to me. Look his eyes just opened and he is trying to speak but I don't understand. It looks like he had some sort of implant in his forehead that is missing. I will swab it with disinfectant."

The stranger sat up, pointed to his ear and said something unintelligible, which they didn't seem to comprehend, so Rodano activated the translator on his belt that Nuptians were required to carry with them at all times in order to communicate with the Centurians.

Again he asked in Nuptian, "Where am I? Who are you? What has happened to me?"

Silence followed for several minutes as the translator ran quick tests with the Chia who repeated words and phrases until finally she nodded her head to Chron, who asked, "Can you understand me now?"

"Yes... at least I believe so. Am I dead?"

Chron laughed, "No you appear to be just as alive as we are and all your gear is safe. You are now in a cave on the asteroid Vesta. My name is Chron. What is yours?"

The stranger cleared his throat and said, "My name is Rodano. I was conducting a gravity wave energy study on my home planet, Nuptia. How did I get here?"

Chron helped Rodano stand and they moved to the radiating three meter circular opening where they gazed in rapture at a vista of a glowing red ocean, deep black sky and a radiating red sun with a white hot corona—just as Rodano had envisioned.

Rodano started to speak, but was interrupted when suddenly the cavern started to vibrate and lights on the mysterious racks of electronic equipment that lined the walls of the room flashed on and off, emitting chirps and beeps. Moments later, the group jumped back and covered their ears as another train thundered past sounding its whistle and towing what appeared to be an open air passenger car packed with people.

Rodano said, "I don't know how, but this must be some sort of deception....or some sort of bad dream. Trains like that carry tourists to Red Cliff Beach on Nuptia. I tried to warn them that dangerous waves were coming, but as usual, I was ignored. It looks like they caught on and are evacuating the beach.

How could I have gotten here in just the blink of an eye?"

"Plus I have no idea of *'when'* is there compared to *'when'* is here."

Chron shrugged. "We don't know either. But it could be that you have entered some sort of hyperspace portal."

Rodano laughed. "Of course that is only conjecture here and now at this time."

Chron shrugged again. "We don't know either. But it could be that we have encountered some sort of hyperspace portal. Of course, that is only conjecture here and now at this time."

Rodano replied, "I see you have a sense of humor which is really rare in my society, but a hyperspace portal? I have theorized that hyperspace transport is theoretically possible and that some offworlders may have developed that capacity, but we have never developed or even encountered an authentic hyperspace system."

Chron offered, "Our home planet is called 'Earth' and we are exploring this asteroid because it obviously seems to have some very unique technology. It also anchors our Space-Hook which is an experiment in which we are sending ice to the tropical Pacific to cool our planet's overheated oceans."

He pointed to each member of the group and spoke their names and areas of expertise, finally ending with Torch who said, "We have spent weeks trying to get into this part of the cave including all sorts of our most advanced drilling and cutting tools without any progress. Somehow the walls are generating oxygen, that's why we aren't wearing space helmets with respirators. We do need them outside. I am sure we can outfit you."

Rodano touched the wall and said, "It doesn't look like any substance that I have had experience with. So how did you get the portal to open?"

Chron replied. "Honestly, we don't know. Madeline has been detecting phenomena that seem connected...and then we have the *Mystery Glove* that may have played some role. Hiroshi and I were starting to X-Ray the glove that we found when it ripped out of my hand and banged off the ceiling. I caught it just before it hit the floor and then I accidentally slipped and knocked my head against the wall right where the portal opened."

Rodano asked, "Did the glove touch the wall?'

Astra said, "I was watching and I think it might have grazed the wall right before this whole massive chamber behind us opened up along with the portal."

"Plus the Alfvén waves that were generating magnetic fields of accelerating electrons waves may have been involved, but that was only a once in a lifetime event. But if I had to guess, I would focus on the glove. Can I see it?"

Hiroshi said, "The wall just slid open to this room and that strange window. We have never even been this far into the cave until now. Our exploration of this cave has just begun, but it looks like this new section is jammed with high tech systems It's going to take a team of our best most brilliant nerds to figure out this mystery."

Chron retrieved the glove from the container on the lab bench and said, "This is how our investigation started. We found this near the mouth of the cave."

He handed it to Rodano who immediately said, "Right hand, six fingers. I believe we have a similar one in our Astro Museum but it is left handed...possibly a mate? No one knows much about it. You figure 'alien', right?"

Chron nodded. "Rodano, assuming that you seem to have arrived here through the portal, will you be anxious to try to return that way back to your home?"

Rodano laughed. "No way. If I go back, I will be arrested and sent to jail...just because I refused to wear a position locator and surveillance unit in my frontal lobe. I would prefer to live here with you in this cave rather than spend another day on Nuptia."

Torch laughed, shook Rodano's hand while slapping him on the back. "Then let me be the first to welcome you to our planet—no eavesdropping required...or even allowed on Earth. Getting you an international Visa may set a precedent."

Chron responded, "As the first New-Human, I can attest to that and I hope that this portal opens up a new future for human exploration and that you are welcome to stay with us as long as you wish."

Astra interjected. "I for one would very much like to analyze your code to see if I can work up your ancestral family tree...if you don't mind?"

Rodano nodded, then laughed. "I would like that. Maybe we are related somehow in the past or maybe even the future."

Chia moved from behind the group to address Rodano. "As Chron mentioned, I am a news reporter and as such always looking for a good story. I can't think of any that might be as exciting as an interview with a with a visitor from another planet. That is if you don't mind all the attention it will likely generate."

FREEDOM RIDE

"Sure, no problem. This is all quite amazing. I had no idea that teleportation was possible when I dropped into a giant wave. It really was a *freedom ride* that I will cherish forever!"

****

Cover Art by Michael H.D. Dormer

****

RON S. NOLAN

Alien Portal?
Mystery Cave?
Mystery Glove?
Hyperspace?
Hyperdrive?

It all continues in book three of the
Metamorphosis Chronicles.

****

If you would like to be notified
when my new novels are published,
send me an e-mail at

nolan@planetropolis.com

(Your contact information will not be shared
with anyone else.)

My website has book descriptions,
interviews and backstories that reveal
some of the amazing adventures
that have shaped my career as
a science fiction writer.

www.planetropolis.com

See you out there....

— *The Elephant* —

I looked forward to enjoying a few weeks off from my marine biology studies in the Hawaiian Islands so it wasn't hard for my old adventure pal, Hollis Robins, to convince me that a visit to Kenya was in order. Especially convincing was his argument that it was "now or never"—the apartheid violence was fire crackling south to north over that volatile continent.

Hollis met me in Nairobi on a blue sky Sunday that could only be described as *'African.'* A quick pass through customs found us at the very prestigious Roberts Brothers Outfitters, where I was soon clothed in true bush fashion. The occasion merited rum tonics at the Fenestrian Club where we became entranced by a golden brown Indian dancer sensuously swaying and glistening in sultry exertion.

Suddenly, an out-of-breath black man, dressed in khaki shorts and trembling with nervous excitement, engaged Hollis in animated mouth-to-ear conversation. In the smoke-dimmed atmosphere of the Fenestrian, I could only make out the terrified look in the black man's eyes.

We settled our tab and retreated to the barely less cacophonous bustle of the side street. Hollis introduced me to Motambu, whom I believe called me "Bwana" in a thick Swahili accent. A hazy reminiscence of intensive archaeological digs in the Olduvai Gorge, big game safaris, and remnants of "Darkest Africa" adventure films sublimated from my memory.

The problem was obviously serious, but neither Hollis nor Motambu took time to translate their animated discourse. I was certain that the mystery of Kenya was sure to be at the heart of it.

Finally, Hollis explained that Motambu's village was in danger. His tribe once lived as nomadic hunters, harvesting the abundant game of the savannas. But since the missionary invasion, they had become chained to the land, nurturing gardens and domestic crops. Now the women covered their breasts and the warriors only attacked the insects which coveted their crops.

A young bull elephant, who once had been considered merely a pest because of his careless excursions through the village had become more than a nuisance. Now he was the enemy. In the early morning hours, he had trampled a hut and killed a sleeping child. The Kenyan Park Service paid little attention to the catastrophe and a few young rebels—dissatisfied with their domesticated lives—began to revive the ancient tribal beliefs about demons and spirits. They claimed that the elephant meant to punish the tribe for so easily relinquishing the ancient traditions of the Serengeti. Although Motambu adamantly professed no belief in the supernatural, his pupils widened when Hollis questioned him about the elephant. Motambu wanted Hollis to kill the elephant and return peace to his people.

We awoke to black coffee at dawn, then drove

directly to the Nairobi gun club to sight in our Weatherby Express rifles. Within two hours we were both cracking the centers from the 500 meter targets and received compliments from the club tenders. This was exciting. I hadn't handled a weapon since Army basic training— when after winning a sharpshooter rating, the military brains assigned me to the important position of Army cook.

The next day, Hollis and Motambu meticulously stowed our camp provisions into the rear compartment of the stubby, silver Land Rover. We had a melange of gear and supplies including spotting scopes, binoculars, ammunition, sleeping bags, maps, rifle cleaning kits game knives and even a set of walkie talkies. The Rover reeked of pungent gun oil and engine exhaust. At the Fenestrian we bought a case of Jamaican rum as "antidote for mosquitoes and leopards."

Just after we had squeezed into our respective niches in the Rover, an impeccably dressed valet from the Nairobi Hilton dashed in front of the Rover and flagged us to a stop. He gave a quick bow and then said, "Important call for Mr. Robbins."

Hollis looked crestfallen when he returned from the hotel lobby. An unexpected and critical business complication demanded his immediate attention and he had to catch the next flight back to his office in London.

Motambu's expression reflected his fading hope. He anxiously offered in broken English, "What about the other Bwana?"

There was no choice. I was to go ahead and Hollis would follow as soon as possible.

With Motambu smiling again at the wheel and me in khaki pants, jacket, and high, brown leather boots, I did feel like a 'Bwana.' The elephant gun between my knees, a 600 DB Express, added to the image. Just three days before, I had been plunging along the leeward side of Molokai Island in my dive skiff, elated at having just completed a three year underwater research study. Now, I felt the same sense of elation, bouncing along the Serengeti plains in a noisy British Land Rover. No matter that Motambu and I shared a scant mutual vocabulary of a handful of words. This was African adventure!

Motambu was obviously pleased as his imagination savored the exorcism of the elephant. His round, black head casually bobbed in tune to the pitching of the Rover over the dirt road.

Facial expressions were my best means of reading the Kenyan's mood and there could be no doubt about Motambu's present optimism when he turned and flashed me a yellow, toothy grin. As I poured a Dixie cup full of brown rum, an uncomfortable thought came to mind. *What if we really do find this rogue elephant? Thanks a lot, Hollis, damn you!*

Many jolting hours later we rattled into a scattered, dusty collection of mud and grass thatched huts–some with rusted tin roofs–just as a wide, flaming disc of red sun descended into a panoramic silhouette of stark thorn trees. The quiet dusk shattered when the village discovered that Motambu had returned with a 'white savior.'

We were inundated by jabbering, curious Kenyans of every size, sex and shape. I felt greatly relieved when a thin young man greeted me in broken English and immediately Djakir's interpretive services were secured.

The elephant had been sighted near the river that

THE ELEPHANT

afternoon only a few miles south of the village. I learned from Djakir that the elephant's terror was not so much in the material beast itself, but in the malignant spirit which held it in its power. Too soon I was to find that the mere skin and bones of the elephant were sufficient cause for concern—no supplemental devil of any sort was necessary.

The next day was uneventful. I delayed stalking the elephant in hopes that Hollis would arrive and take over the marauder's eradication. Djakir and Motambu patiently coached me in elephantology, while I humored their efforts, knowing that Hollis would soon take charge.

The next day was spent like the former. Because there still had been no word from Hollis, I continued stalling for time while Motambu had lost his proud bearing and had begun avoiding the questioning glances of his compatriots. The tribe seemed to think it might have invested false hope in their white savior. I still hadn't confessed that my hunter forte was limited to reef fish and a hand spear.

The atmosphere became dismal; charged conversations took place just beyond my earshot. I imagined the general consensus to be, *"Let's get this ordeal over with, so we can get on with our lives, crops and children. Why won't the Bwana kill the demon?"*

Around midnight, the elephant ransacked a supply hut on the periphery of the village. Luckily no one was injured, but the sphere of the elephant's life and mine had suddenly and irrevocably engaged. *He must be killed and I am the one that must do it.*

No sleep came for me following the attack, and the dark hours were spent in meticulously breaking down, cleaning and oiling the massive Express rifle. My mind wandered halfway around the world to my Honolulu home and to the sleek, young fashion designer whom I had met only two weeks ago. *She must be touching up her impeccable tan in front of the Royal Hawaiian at Waikiki*, I speculated. When I phoned to break our second date, she choked, "Africa? What are you going to do in Africa?" I didn't know then, but I could reply now, *Shoot a rogue elephant and save a village.*

We parked the Rover at the base of a jagged canyon about a mile downstream from the elephant's watering hole. The plan was to sneak up to the villain while he was drinking or lounging on the warm mud banks.

We carefully tested the wind direction to avoid alerting the elephant's uncanny sense of hearing and smell and it took us an hour to carefully maneuver into position.

With a great lump in my throat, I went ahead to peer over the canyon edge and blast the elephant. My mind echoed, *"Get this over with and get back to our lives, crops and children."* I tried to be composed and coached myself that there was no danger and only one shot would be needed.

I mechanically inched forward on knees and elbows toward the edge of the cliff with binoculars held aloft in one hand and the elephant gun in the other. I carefully oh–so carefully, approached the vantage point. Placing the Express securely at my side, I took off my hat and listened to the blood and adrenaline cascading through my ears and temples. With consciously measured control, I looked down at the muddy watering pool and held the weapon at the ready. The soft mud banks were stamped with a confused pattern of oval footprints—but there was no elephant. The thick, opaque stream drifted unconcernedly beneath my rifle sights as if it already knew that there was to be no bloodshed there today.

I hoarsely called to the others and noted the sad disappointment in their eyes. "Not here, Bwana?" asked Djakir.

We squatted and looked down upon the tropical, green valley slashed by the meandering, chocolate stream. While Motambu began planning our next move, Djakir explained that he and I must return to the Rover and drive up to the next pool. Motambu meanwhile, would continue tracking the elephant on foot.

"It would have to be this way," I thought. *'I must meet the enemy in his environment, challenge him on his own terms for his crimes against the village."*

****

As we approached the rendezvous point, we met Motambu who was waving his arms in frenzied excitement.

Djakir explained, "He has found fresh elephant sign and we must go...now!"

The trail was considerably more recent than even Motambu had hoped, because we suddenly discovered the elephant only 600 meters ahead. His back was to us and he was struggling for a purchase near the base of a small thorn tree. As he backed away, his trunk drew taut and the tree resoundingly popped from the ground spraying dirt from its severed roots.

We squatted in the waist-high, yellow-green sea of coarse grass as I hurriedly fumbled for two of the brass-cased rounds which decorated my hunting jacket. In spite of my trembling fingers, the shells reluctantly entered the rifle's chamber. I left Djakir and Motambu and stalked—crouched and hidden by the swaying vegetation.

I was clearly on my own. There was no thought of Hollis, Motambu or Djakir or even of the village children. The only essence was that of the prey; he was still unaware that I was stalking him. The trial had begun.

I paused to calculate the distance to the target, which still gave no sign that danger approached. I moved in fifty more meters and then forced myself to wait until my exploding lungs quieted.

I could delay no more with the Express seated firmly against my shoulder, I swept the grass down with a fast sweep of my left arm. As soon as the front sight and the rear sight aligned, I drew a bead directly into the kill zone of the elephant. I touched up the aim and precisely squeezed off one barrel, then corrected and fired the next. The reports were violent and shocking in the quiet, hushed valley. I stood full up as the elephant turned toward me, at first with surprise, then in rage. He raised his slender trunk, peeled his ears forward and backward, and shrieked a cry of alarm—then challenge.

HE CHARGED! Slowly at first, but with amazing acceleration. Time stopped for me. I knew that my shots were sound, but they seemed to have had no effect on the beast. *Maybe they had missed after all?*

Panicked, I fumbled with another heavy bullet, trying to jam it into the left chamber. Suddenly, the blast furnace thundering of the elephant drowned out the roar of my racing heart and I knew he was only meters away.

"Keep it together," I demanded my stiff fingers. The

oiled Express action snapped tight. I smoothly lifted the rifle and fired point blank into the elephant's left eye, directly into his brain case. A spring of thick blood and grey matter erupted from the eye.

The elephant abruptly halted his charge, almost as if he had suddenly decided to become friends. His head swiveled so that his right, good eye could take me in and he seemed to be on the verge of resuming his charge.

During this frozen moment, the young bull's thoughts turned within as he slowly and sadly bowed to his heavy knees. He courageously attempted a last echoing trumpet now just barely able to pull his leaden trunk over his head. His haunting bellow said farewell to the savanna that he loved and to a soon hoped for mate. His hind legs folded and he collapsed falling heavily on his side. His breath became blood–raspy, halting and pained.

I cautiously approached the heaving backside of this once proud monarch. His good eye reflected the delicate acacias; the cerulean sky filled with tumbling, iridescent clouds and the lush greenness of the sweet grass. He showed no fear when I positioned the muzzle next to his remaining eye. It fixed on mine as the rifle discharge relieved him from his agony.

As his vision left him, so did mine. With uncontrollable tears, I slumped against his magnificent body and relived the melancholy of his last trumpet. That sadness drowned out the jubilance and glee of the chattering Motambu and Djakir who were dancing around the elephant, crazily leaping from his back and fearlessly pulling his tail.

RON S. NOLAN

The Elephant Backstory

When I lived in Honolulu, Hawaii in the mid seventies, a South African girl introduced me to her friend Eric Rundgren who was visiting the islands on vacation. I was amazed at meeting the famous safari hunter since the month before I had written "The Elephant." As I recollect, he said he really liked the story and that it was "believable"...or something to that effect.

As we patronized several bars in downtown Honolulu, Eric reminisced that he shared Ernest Hemingway's fondness for big game safaris in Africa. Little did I know then, but soon after I was to become good friends and fishing buddies with Ernest's son, Jack Hemingway and his daughter Margeux. In the spring of 1989, I produced a film that starred Jack flyfishing in the Florida Keys and in 1990 attended Jack's wedding in Ketchum, Idaho.

Hot Night in Kansas

1967

After three summer months in San Francisco—aka *The City*—where Jimmy had lived in a Haight–Ashbury commune and where he had experienced the mystic hippie lifestyle: letting his hair grow, smoking weed, experiencing free love, hanging out with flower people and immensely enjoying concerts at the Fillmore Auditorium where he rocked out to the Doors, Fleetwood Mac, Richie Havens and Country Joe and the Fish.

He had navigated the Bay Area in a Ford Fairlane which was a surprise gift from his stepfather who was a successful romance novel author living in Boulder with one of his former, female grad students.

It all started in the spring when Jimmy was winding up his senior year at Kaw River High in Olathe, Kansas and had fallen head over heels in love with one of his classmates. His mother didn't seem to care much and it looked like Jimmy might elope and get hitched—much to the concern of his stepfather who felt that Jimmy should hold off for a while. So even though his stepfather no longer lived with Jimmy's mom, he cared about Jimmy and his future and had mailed Jimmy a train ticket to Denver where they met and his stepfather had surprised him with an envelope containing keys to a bright red one year old Ford Fairlane, a Phillips gas card and $1,000 in cash for food and sodas. He also gave him the names and phone numbers of his former students who now worked for newspapers and magazines in the Bay Area.

Jimmy figured that the present was an attempt to make up for the stress his stepdad had caused when his mom had caught him sleeping with another woman. The irony was that his stepdad had sponsored Jimmy's trip to give Jimmy time to reconsider his plan to marry a very smart and a real beauty of a girl from Topeka who had just turned eighteen and who had called Jimmy every day asking him to please come home. Although Jimmy told her that he wanted to become a writer and was doing research for a story about the Bay Area lifestyle, Sonya threatened to sever their relationship if he wasn't back soon!

So here he was, long hair flapping in the breeze, wearing a colorful tie dyed t-shirt and listening to rock music on the radio...reluctantly heading home. Every once in a while, he thought about turning around and going back to California, but he would look at the picture of Sonya taped to the dash and push the gas pedal a little harder.

The problem was that she had a scholarship to attend Kansas University and they would be moving to Lawrence two weeks before the fall semester began. So Jimmy had a job set up at the Army Surplus Store in downtown Lawrence where he would work eight hour shifts, five days a week selling jeans, boots and whatever the owner could put in stock.

And it was hot! Even at night, it was hot! So it was

refreshing to let the big '66 Ford Fairlane. which lacked an AC unit, slow way down as it reached the rare dip in the road on the flat country highway. Just a few feet of lower elevation turned hot and muggy to fresh and cool—then they were back again on the steaming asphalt as they climbed back up—which even at ten o'clock at night was still blistering hot. Kansas in July was a fire breathing dragon. Bigger than big and hotter than hot, except for the occasional gully respite on this long, lonely country blacktop.

For twenty-seven straight hours, the Fairlane had rolled directly from San Francisco to western and now to eastern Kansas. For the last six hours, he had the AM radio set to KOMA in Oklahoma City, 92.5 MHz on the dial. Late at night they had a revival program that sold glow-in-the-dark plastic Jesus's for your dashboard. The Fairlane had one and on the back bumper was pasted a sticker that said, "Red Dog Inn, Lawrence, Kansas" that Sonya had sent him as a present..and reminder?

At Wichita, Jimmy left I-35 and entered the Kansas Turnpike which had a max speed limit of eighty mph, but many v8's going ninety to a hundred. Minimum speed sixty mph. The new law let you drive in the smooth, less used left lane to take the strain off the right lane. It was easy for the Fairlane heading home to easily cruise up to a hundred or so, but still the Kansas Highway Patrol kept passing the Ford like she was at sixty five—and on the right before Jimmy could see them in the rear view mirror and move over.

Having enough of the turnpike and running low on dough, the 175 miles from Wichita to Topeka cost nearly seven dollars and fifty cents, the Fairlane took the exit at Topeka onto the 'old' road to Olathe which sported two rough, dark lanes. Topeka is an Indian word for *'a good place to dig potatoes.'* So most Lawrence college students called it *'Potato Town.'*

At midnight on a Tuesday night there were no other cars, trucks, or road bikes on the highway. But there was still a shade of blue black cotton clouds in the tinge of grey sky lit by a yellow crescent moon rising over the rolling hills.

The Fairlane easily took to the lone highway and went back to a relaxing fifty-five. Mostly it was quite dark except for the car's high beams that illuminated streams of jagged barbwire along each side of the highway. The fence posts, some made of makeshift tree branches leaning to and fro, others stiff green iron slats that whipped as they sped by, kept the Fairlane out and the livestock in.

The bumpy road led the path into the blackness. Above the first bright stars cast shimmerirrg reflections in the Fairlane's deep lacquered, crimson hood. The chrome leaping deer hood ornament gleamed like a diamond fawn while the tires made a black sucking, swishing sound on the warm asphalt. Ahead, the road was lit by the car's bright sweeping headlight cones and behind a blood red glow from its tail lights. The Fairlane was comfortably on course and the road measured up to its sixty's image of a lone country road on a dark country night.

All four windows were cranked down and hot, wet air cruised and buffeted around interior and turbulently escaped leaving room for more hot, dry air. A dull, yellow glow radiated from the AM radio and the speedometer's red needle indicated a steady speed of fifty-five. Old classic, romantic songs were playing softly—mostly they were love songs for those lucky couples who were parking on wooded lanes, wheat fields, and in abandoned driveways and were feeling something that was pretty wild and terrific and potentially serious and possibly illegal on the boy's part.

The Fairlane's driver was heading home to his girl and even though they were both just seniors in high school, he was going to propose marriage. He had had enough of what everyone said...things like *'Think it over stupid. You are way to young to get married.'*

Last week spent with his stepdad in Denver before heading home had not changed his mind. His life was his own and his girl was to become his wife.

Still, he realized that the miles were sublimating and he was nearing his goal. He eased the Fairlane back to forty-five, *'What the hell, there's nobody around. I can go as slow as I want.'* He knew she would be waiting for him at her parents tract house near the Kroger store and she knew he was coming. He wanted her because he loved her. His missing dad was probably part of the reason. His mom never knew how to do anything fun after he died—particularly outdoors where he felt his best. She preferred to stay in her bedroom. *Maybe I want Sonya because I am afraid to be alone?*

For the last half hour, the most that the headlights had shown were endless trains of barbed wire. There was a railroad crossing coming up that he knew on the route and hadn't bothered to slow the Fairlane as they rumbled over the rails. But...something about the endless chain of fields and fences made him worry that he could be passing by somewhere he might or should have been...or want to be or could be still.

A week of the high life with his stepdad in Denver—playing golf at the Evergreen Club and day hiking the picturesque trails in Vail had made him ready for the future. Interestingly enough, now that he had taken the summer off to think things over and be sure of his decisions, his stepdad had approved of Jimmy's marriage.

As Jimmy loaded the Fairlane for the drive home, his stepdad had said, "Your life profession is yours to choose, Jimmy, but I believe that you would make a great author. Write some stories and send them to me if you wish. I would be happy to be your coach."

Jimmy turned off the tunes. The big tires and big engine made little noise at forty-five mph. He stretched his arm out into the warm breeze. They went down through another gully which was cool again for a couple of minutes. Then it was sweltering hot again. The headlights flashed a rhythm on the blacktop and he felt a loneliness tingle his heart and pushed the Fairlane up to 55 mph.

A very long way down the road there was a dim light. As he approached, he could see that the light was on the right side of the highway. Fairly close now, he could see tall oak trees in full dark, green leafage in the moonlight. A way up the gravel road there was a single story, white farm house. Adjacent were corrals and trees and a pond next to a barn twice as big as the house surrounded by farm implements, chicken and pig yards, horses standing next to the fence, milk cows resting in the dirt and bails of alfalfa hay ready to be stored in the barn.

Radiant light from a Coleman lantern silhouetted a bent over farmer and his wife and two children seated at a table in the kitchen...maybe reading the Bible and praying...hoping for rain...listening to the commodities report on the radio before getting an early start—the daily life of a farmer. The Fairlane pulled over and stopped, somehow the lonely light and the family hovering in its glow turned his heart. The farm family gathered at the window, uncertain if they were getting an unexpected visitor. They waved at Jimmy and he waved back and headed back down the road.

He did feel loneliness, but such sweet comfort for the children to be close at home with their parents. When he was their age, he remembered going upstairs to his room with calico curtains and a father who held his shoulder with great love and rough calluses on his hands and wished him a good sleep, "Because you will need your strength tomorrow, my son to help your grandma plant the strawberries in the garden and gather eggs that the hens laid overnight! When you finish, the butter churn needs cranking for the pancakes that you love so much."

But a year later, his birth father had died in an airplane crash on the family's wheat farm in western Kansas in the middle of nowhere. *Would that be my destiny? Is that what bothers me so much about farm life?*

Now barely at forty mph the Fairlane drifted lazily from lane to lane.

A few miles up ahead there was another dull, lonely glow. *"No"* he shouted to no one but the Fairlane, *I won't be a farmer. I must write about the world. I won't stay here and grow plants to feed us and our animals. It hurts too much. The loneliness hurts my soul."*

Tears flooded his eyes as he tromped the Fairlane's accelerator and flashed by the farm, but had to jam on the brakes as he entered the outskirts of Olathe and navigated down the familiar two way street full of red, yellow and green lights and stop signs to his girls parent's house. She had been pacing her room when she saw the Fairlane pull up and park and rushed breathlessly out to meet him. Not bothering to wipe the tears from his eyes, he proposed to her leaning against the Fairlane while her parents watched from the living room window.

Sonya thought he was crying because he loved her. Only he and the Fairlane really knew why.

****

"Mr. Scott's body was lodged in the plane and it was necessary to use cutting torches to free it. Both planes crashed within a block's distance of Roland Scott's home."

Western Times, Tuesday, May 4th, 1950

Roland Scott, Jr. and Marion
Louise Graves
prior to their marriage.

EARTH BOY

2047 Europa
Stage 2 Terraforming

T he small Earth boy wiggled and thrashed impatiently in his suspended, bare wooden crib which to him was an infinity above the ground. One day he was riding in a rocket with his mon, then he woke up somewhere else that he did not know.

He had already, as the blur of light and darkness went on and on, become familiar with the escape mechanism of his aerial prison. When one of the large ones he called them the *'Big Ones'*, pressed something out of his reach, the side wall would descend and they would pull him to the ground and give him a bottle of vile mucousy fluid that made him throw up—still it was better than nothing, he guessed. If he cried, they slapped him, but not too hard to really hurt. At first, one of the Big Ones was nearly always around him, taking turns watching in the dark and light, but this had changed now.

At sporadic and mostly unpredictable times they would encourage him to stumble around for a while on his unsteady, chubby legs until for no apparent reason they would gently coax him back into his isolated compartment which was perched on stilts—perhaps to get rid of him and put him to back to sleep and that was it! They only came back he guessed when they wanted to amuse themselves by bugging him and they often acted unpredictably and spoke very loudly and coarsely.

Hours and hours and minutes and hours would go and not go by and the Big Ones would or would not return. They could or could not be in a particularly friendly or sympathetic or non-sympathetic mood to his imprisonment and the small Earth boy's inability to control his locomotor limbs, bladder and, in no way mentally or physically, able to communicate with the Big Ones..

It seemed to the small Earth boy that he had been so agile, adept and daring before all of this nightmare of imprisonment and was now mired in a slag pile of heavy frustration, However, occasionally, and always with great delight, a small brown, soft, warm being (which the small Earth boy called *'Ranger'* appeared after the cold early morning times were displaced by warm afternoon sunshine.

Ranger had a joyous and devoted interest in the small Earth boy which was often manifested in the copious emission of spurts of saliva and general rough housing—that is during times when the small Earth boy had been granted a temporary leave of absence from prison and permission to play on the scratchy, sand covered flooring

Now every new light period, Ranger would jump up to the small Earth boy's prison wall and shake the whole confinement with his friendly breathing and vibrant tall waggling. The boy loved this intelligent and fur covered individual and actually thought that

EARTH BOY

Ranger loved him too and was trying to get him out of prison. and save him from...and that he and Ranger had been friends and very close a long time before all this consternation with the Big Ones had even started.

He was very sure that some day Ranger was going to free him from the Big Ones that alternately demonstrated kindness and then became touchy and hostile resulting in freedom followed by confinement and confinement followed by freedom and who made hurtful, loud noises and emitted sharp smells.

The small Earth boy was confused and irked, irked and confused. He was not the dumb grub slug that the Big Ones thought that he was. He knew a lot and he had been a lot of places and seen a lot of things. But he felt groggy, like he was underwater and just coming up for air—just like he had been when he had seen the first Big One and the second Big One—the mean one in a white suit that struck him from behind just as he got his first breath of this heavy air here, wherever here was now.

He longed to go back to before and back to where he kind of remembered that those there spoke freely and never imprisoned anyone and he was sort of more like a Big One type than Ranger. But every day he lay tn his inaccessible island, unable to control his digestive tract, unable to feed himself and totally dependent upon one of the Big One's sacs of fluid.. he remembered less and less... and became more frightened ...and felt more alone.

Ranger was his best and only friend. He slowly remembered and rapidly forgot a glorious time before his first contact and subsequent confinement with the Big Ones. As he was remembering less and less and becoming more and more confused by the strange behavior of the Big Ones, Ranger became more and more like a constant, welcome companion. He watched over the small Earth boy as time rhythmically slid from light to dark and dark to light.

The Big Ones came and shared their sacs of warm mucous and cleaned the Earth boy's bottom and spoke to him in some sort of alien tongue...some of which seemed less and less alien and more and more familiar every time they spewed forth.

One early, grey light period Ranger did not show. Thoughts and more thoughts and missing and wondering and wiggles and stretches and harsh throat sounds over and over and over and there was no Ranger.

The small Earth boy was stressed and worried that the Big Ones had imprisoned Ranger in a stilt island like his and that he would never see Ranger again—unless he could escape his captors

He waited and waited, trying not to believe this and his thoughts of before as the Big Ones became deeper underwater and harder and much harder to fathom.

He had no choice but to try to decipher the code of the Big Ones so he could learn how to lower his prison wall and find a way of rescuing Ranger—his only ally.

The Big Ones seemed confused, but admittedly somewhat interested in his attempts to use sign language and percussion code with a hollow plastic, shot filled device they had rattled into his prison. Nevertheless, he picked up upon sounds that they continuously emitted full of vapor and mouth warmth...sounds sprayed and slurred from their faces.

He feared that Ranger might not take to confinement as well as he had and he rasped and grunted one code sound similar to one that the Big Ones frequently uttered and that he hoped might someday aid his escape.

It was a simple sonorous communication that sounded like "da da" (lower pitch) and "da da" (higher pitch) and repeated twice as a signature musical note sound that he seemed to hear frequently when the Big Ones let him out of his prison cell.

Immediately one of the Big Ones (the one without the feeding sacs) repeated the notes and carefully extracted the small Earth boy from his cell and raised him high in the air and repeated the notes followed by loud wet sounds of great happiness about the small Earth boy's ability to decipher the Big One's code for release from the torture of imprisonment

However, due to the Big One's inadvertent pressure, the little Earth boy suffered an embarrassing and unexpected impact upon his lower unit resulting in a stream of diarrhea ran onto the floor and an over-whelming nasty smell that was not at all hygienic in nature or substance which the other Big Once removed with some sort of energized mop and made sounds that could possibly have been their version of laughter.

The small Earth boy now realized that he might be able to acquire his freedom by appeasing the Big Ones with the most simplistic of maneuvers.

So...the small Earth Boy repeated the "da da's" several times, each time pausing for a breath. Now the Big Ones joined in and began moving their arms in synchrony to the sounds. *Could they be dancing?* thought the Earth Boy as they left the room, granting the small Earth Boy his freedom.

The Earth Boy thought, "The Big Ones let me out so now I can find Ranger. He must know how we can get out of here and back home. Wherever that is.

He yelled enthusiastically, "da da...da da! It works, yes, da da!"

****

Earth Space Force Captain Sheila Garson, an accomplished shuttle pilot and navigator was sitting dejected in the hot sun that was baking the red-hued valley. She used her arm to brush the mix of sweat and tears from her eyes and was amazed to see her missing dog dragging a makeshift sled constructed of tree branches bearing a small child that was crying "Mommy! Mommy!"

She ran to the sled just as the Earth Boy pulled himself upright, and awkwardly tried to run towards his mother, but was just starting to fall as his mother bent down and swept him upwards and swirled him around in welcome home exuberance.

"Oh my God! Richie is it you? Oh my baby, are you OK? It has been three—no four weeks since you disappeared. I wish Ranger could talk and tell us where you have been. I know that the 'red heelers' are very intelligent canines, but Ranger... you are our hero! I am so glad that the Space Force assigned you to us."

Ranger ignored the captain as he lapped water and gobbled pellets from bowls in his kennel. When he came out and sat by her side, Sheila continued. "Thank you Ranger for bringing Richie home!"

She looked at Richie who was standing next to Ranger, stoking his forehead.

"Son, I should never have left you in the shuttle, but I decided that I needed to climb that cliff to enhance our SOS signal which I thought was being blocked by heavy elements in the soil here in the valley. I was only going to be gone for a few minutes, so it didn't seem dangerous since we haven't seen anyone else since we landed here."

Richie was looking intensely at the dog while listening to his mother who continued. "I couldn't carry you and the heavy gear that I needed, but when I came back, both of you were gone. I have been searching desperately every day since, but I did fix the fuel transfer problem so we are ready to fly back to Earth."

She took Richie to his sleeping quarters where she began wiping his face with a wet towel.

She asked, "How have you been surviving all this time? Are you hungry? My breasts are full of milk."

She unzipped her top and held Richie close and he began nursing feverishly humming "da da...da da."

Suddenly he stopped, opened his eyes wide and vomited in her lap.

RACE DAY IN ALABAMA

Narration with Flashbacks

Race Day Pre-Race Show
NRL Championship
Huntsville Raceland Speedway
Huntsville, Alabama
Sunday, November 16, 2008

I n the broadcast booth with a panorama of the track in the background, Jack Kelly and color commentator, Larry Jenkins are announcing the last race of season. Jack says that the last two weeks have been bizarre and that it is a testimony to National Racing League (NRL) President Ray Jones that this race is even being held.

Larry agrees and points out that the championship is up in the air and will be decided today. After a season of thirty-five races, only five points separate the leader, Jim Chapet, from Tony, *'the Tornado'* Garland. The standings could not be much closer. It all boils down to this; if Chapet wins the race, he wins the championship. If Chapet comes in second and leads the most laps and Garland comes in first, they will both end the season with 6,600 points and there will be a split championship. For Garland to win the championship, he needs to win the race plus either prevent Chapet from coming in second or logging the most led laps.

Larry notes that way down in the 23rd position, there is a newcomer to the roster named 'Bobby Wilson, Jr.' from Lost River, Texas, who is running his first NRL race. If it had not been for one the drivers being hospitalized during practice, Jr. would most likely be watching this race on TV, not making his debut in the NRL season finale. Larry calls up a clip of a pre-race interview in which Junior credits Bob Werner of Werner Racing with giving him a chance. Larry remarks about how much Jr. looks just like his dad did at the same age.

Kansas State Speedway
Topeka, Kansas
Four Years Earlier

Two close friends from grade school through adult life have competed in racing from go karts to stock cars. Ray Jones is successful and on his way to his third NRL championship. He commutes to race events in his own private jet. In contrast, Bobby Wilson has barely won enough NRL races to stay in the game, but he has yet to make the big-time. As Ray's success grows, Bobby's jealousy and resentment fester. And as Bobby falls farther and farther behind in the race standings, he spends more and more late nights in race town bars and dives.

Bobby takes out his frustration by driving aggres-
sively, drawing complaints from other drivers, and
reprimands and fines from the league officials. In
Kansas at the last race of the season, he must place in
the top ten to keep his sponsorship, but he is having a
miserable run and is about to be lapped by the car
running in second place driven by a young hot shot,
Sam Strong, a rookie that has just recently jumped
from sprint to stock cars. Bobby's spotter tells him to
go low and let Strong swing ahead.

Bobby ignores his spotter and holds his line. Sam
tries to go high, but Bobby drifts up the track. Then
Sam tries the bottom lane. Bobby blocks him. Bobby's
pit chief radios him that NRL wants him to let the
faster Strong go by, but Bobby refuses. Sam purposely
brakes late into turn four, builds up momentum,
swings back down to the bottom of the track and
punches Bobby in the rear, a classic 'bump and run'
spinning Bobby around and pushing him out of the
way. Fortunately Bobby doesn't hit any of the other
cars which slide every direction in clouds of black
smoke. The yellow caution flag is raised and Bobby
heads down pit road with a flat tire, fuming mad!

After the pit crew fuels the car and changes all four
tires, the crew chief jabs his index finger at Bobby's
forehead: the message is to start thinking. It's like
pouring gasoline on Bobby's burning anger. He peels
out, fishtailing out of his pit box. Now he is at the back
of the pack and two laps down.

The green flag drops. Bobby quickly accelerates but
the spin has knocked the front wheels out of align-

ment. The steering wheel vibrates like a paint shaker and he can barely stay off the wall in the turns. He sees Ray, the leader, fast growing larger in his rear view mirror. He grudgingly moves over to let him pass.

And then he sees Sam Strong right on his rear bumper. Sam knocks him just like before, but this time, Bobby's car slides backwards up the track and smashes hard into the wall bringing out another yellow caution.

Bobby is finished for the day, the season and his career is likely over as well. His hands are trembling with rage when he waves away the paramedic trying to pull down the window net. He restarts the engine and joins in the cue, holding out his hand signaling that he is heading for pit road.

Since the race had only progressed five laps since the last caution, the rest of the pack is staying out. Furious, Bobby enters pit road, showering sparks from the undercarriage and spewing smoke from a rubbing tire. He hesitates for an instant then drives right past the turnoff leading to the garage. He suddenly accelerates down pit road, roaring past his crew members frantically waving at him from track side. The radio query from his pit chief goes unanswered. Suddenly Bobby speeds onto the track and 'T-bones' Sam ramming his car up the track and into the wall. Bobby is knocked unconscious, Sam is awake but severely injured; he will never walk again!

Sam and the District Attorney want to charge Bobby with attempted manslaughter, but the investigation conducted by the NRL calls it an 'accident,' that Bobby's earlier wreck had jammed the throttle linkage and that the engine showed signs of over revving. The investigators were unable to say with any certainty whether the malfunction had occurred before their final encounter or earlier when Sam had spun Bobby into the wall. The case is dropped, but Bobby loses his primary sponsor and then without notice, his wife runs off with another guy leaving Bobby to raise their twelve year old girl Katie and eight year old boy Bobby Jr on his own.

Blackballed by car owners and sponsors, Bobby is through as a driver. He takes his last pay check and with $26,000 in savings packs up his RV and heads back to Lost River, Texas, his birthplace. He gets a $100,000 bank loan to buy a rundown 500 acre, mesquite-ridden ranch and, with the help of a borrowed bobcat and road grader, puts in the county's first and only automobile race track,—a mile long oval dirt track and inner track for go karts, monster trucks, figure eight races, and demolition derby's.

At first, the seating consists only of bring-your-own lawn chairs and the race cars are nothing but second rate junkers. In the second season Bobby puts in bleachers and a concession operation, adds fence barriers around the main track and officially gets a business license and permit to operate the track. Bobby dreams someday of building a state-of-the-art mile and a half long, concrete surface super speedway

Race Day–Race Start—Lap 1/300
Huntsville Raceland Speedway

RACE DAY IN ALABAMA

Huntsville, Alabama

The green flag drops and the long awaited NRL championship race for 2008 is underway! Tony Garland in the pole position takes the lead, Jim Chapet falls smoothly behind into second place. The pack moves up to full speed. Chapet's crew chief radios him that it was a good start and to just stay cool.

Suddenly there is trouble in the back of the pack. The number 19 car spins its wheels and loses traction. The cars behind expecting to accelerate are late in checking up. Bobby Jr narrowly misses the car in front of him by dodging down to the apron. His spotter compliments him on avoiding a wreck. Out comes the yellow flag.

Lost River Racetrack
Lost River, Texas
August 9th 1993

On race nights, the Lost River track is beginning to draw more fans and now a few semi-pro racers are showing up. The Lost River High School auto mechanics class has developed a waiting list of kids wanting to race-modify anything on wheels. But money is as always tight and Bobby takes on construction work during the week. But with the responsibility of raising Katie and Bobby Jr he is getting further and further in debt and more depressed. He drinks a fifth of Jack Daniels every night and shows it in the mornings.

Bobby's once-best-friend Ray, now known as 'Big Ray," has worked his way up from driver to team owner, and then eventually goes on to becoming the president and major shareholder of the NRL.

Meanwhile Bobby is in a death spiral. spending most nights with the other regulars at Lost River's one and only dive leaving Katie to take care of Bobby Jr. Katie keeps food on the table by working after school at a clothing store. Even with all of her burdens at home, Katie excels in high school and qualifies for the accelerated program for college aspirants. A pretty brunette with a nice figure, she has no time for dates and is completely focused on her studies. Her goal is to be accepted by an accredited college that offers courses on the Internet. She has her sights on a degree in law.

By the age of fourteen, Bobby Jr has learned a lot about life, like stay away from dad if he has been drinking. Sister Katie is really more like a mom than a sister to him and even though she has little enthusiasm for racing, she helps him pay for his go kart and racing jacket, shoes and parts. Lost River is his home track, but there are occasional forays to races in south Texas and Oklahoma City, all of which Katie somehow finds a way to finance.

Still Bobby Jr never finishes higher than third in any race, something always seems to happen. He wonders if he is jinxed. Tony Garland, a boy his age from Silverstone 30 miles away, always aces him out in the end.

RACE DAY IN ALABAMA

Tony is an arrogant bully, but Tony's older brother, Jay Garland is a good guy. He teaches auto mechanics at the high school and works at an auto parts and speed equipment shop on weekends where Bobby Jr. is a regular customer. To his younger brother's irritation, Jay even helps Bobby Jr. work on his cart after school and during races if Junior's dad is too hung over.

Bobby Jr. knows that Jay has been hot for his sister Katie since she was a freshman and Jay was a senior in high school. She is friendly to him, but never accepts his invitations for anything except a rare church social or one of Bobby Jr's races.

Race Day–Lap 31/300
Huntsville Raceland Speedway
Huntsville, Alabama

Jack Kelly reports that there is more trouble on the backstretch, another caution flag is out. The leaders seem able to quickly pull out front on restarts, but the pack is totally jammed up and is one huge wreck waiting to happen. The number 39 and 27 cars have collided.

One driver is transported to the track medical center. Kelly notes that rookie, Bobby Jr has moved up from 23rd to 18th and that, if he can stay out of trouble, he might do all right in his first race.

Farm Fair Racetrack
Oklahoma City, Oklahoma
June 5th, 1994

Katie sits, fidgeting in the bleachers at a dry, dusty dirt track in northern Oklahoma on a blistering hot summer Sunday afternoon nervously rooting for Junior in his bright silver 35 horse power go kart who is leading the pack on the next to the last lap of the season's final race. Suddenly, the red kart in second place rams Bobby Jr sending him bouncing off course and into the infield tire barrier.

Katie rushes over to her brother, but Bobby Jr pushes her away shouting that he is OK. Then he yanks off his helmet and slams it into the dirt, storming off towards Tony who had blind-sided him. Katie grabs his arm, swings him around and sternly suggests that they load up so she can get back to writing the brief that she has to turn in the next morning for the online course that she is taking from the University of Texas School of Law.

On the road, Bobby Jr moans that he never has any luck, that there is always something that breaks, or he runs out of gas, or he gets bushwhacked. Katie suggests that he take up another sport, like model airplanes, or video games, but they both know that racing is in his blood.

Race Day–Lap 96/300
Huntsville Raceland Speedway
Huntsville, Alabama

Jack Kelly comments that Tony Garland and Jim Chapet continue to battle it out for the lead. After a scheduled green flag pit stop, Chapet is first out of his pit box and accelerates down pit road and onto the track. The leaders are almost five seconds ahead of the third place car. Larry Jenkins reports that Bobby Jr is still advancing, now in 12th position and that it would be a real win for Junior if he finishes in the top ten in his first NRL race.

Lost River Racetrack
Lost River, Texas
September, 15th, 1996

Bobby Jr has jumped from go karts to sprint cars and, after a long series of no finishes in the top ten, is finally making some progress. He has scored a couple of thirds, one second, and a first at the Wyandotte Half Mile Sprint Race—his first time to finish a race as the leader. He feels that his luck has changed and even his sister is somewhat encouraged.

Katie, now "Kate" since she graduated and passed the Texas bar exam with one of the top scores, is fidgeting again. Just as Bobby Jr's sprint car slides around turn four of the Lost River track, his right front wheel flies off and sails over the fence into the stands; the car digs into the dirt and rolls over and over out of control. The yellow flag is out. Kate is on the track and rushes to the wreck. Junior's car is upside down and severely damaged. Jay Garland is already at the scene, single handedly trying to turn the car over. Fuel is leaking and making a puddle in the red dirt. A para-medic yells at Kate to stay back— they have to turn the car over and fast! In spite of the warning to stay clear, Kate helps Jay and several course workers flip the car right side up.

Bobby Jr is unconscious. The paramedics pull him from the car and load him in the ambulance. Kate and Jay insist upon riding along. Junior wakes up and asks what happened. Jay explains that he lost a wheel in the turn. The paramedic says he can't find any broken bones or concussion, that he got off easy. Junior asks Jay how the friggin' wheel could come off. Jay shrugs and says that he will check it out.

NRL Headquarters
Memphis, Tennessee
November, 1st 2000

Samuel Strong grits his teeth and rolls his wheel chair through the door held open by the pretty receptionist at NRL headquarters. He mentally compares her to his wife, an elegant rose of blond curls and blue eyes and decides Nancy wins again. Although their sex life ceased with his wreck, she still remains with him and seems to be happy enough. Sam doesn't mind if she has other friends—as long as they are women. Money is no problem; his old friend Ray Jones, now the NRL CEO, kindly offered him a job in the finance department and Sam has been promoted to Vice President and is happy as a person confined to a wheel chair could be.

The meeting between Big Ray and Sam is to strategize the expansion of the league into the state of Texas. The NRL has only one track in the entire state, the Dallas Oval. Ray wants another and wants it fast for two reasons. The first is a result of nature. Because of the five hundred million dollar cost of rebuilding Padre

RACE DAY IN ALABAMA

Island due to the devastation from the last hurricane, the state budget is way in the red. Big Ray has been tipped off that two key state legislators are planning to propose a significant tax on revenues from any new race tracks built in Texas.

Shrewd businessmen and political power brokers, the state politicians realize that stock car racing is not only extremely lucrative, but one of the fastest growing sports in the world. And they figure that the NRL plans to build more tracks in Texas.

The second reason is also based upon inside information. Since Big Ray is a major contributor to the political establishment in Washington, D.C., he's been tipped off that Congress is preparing to award Newton Enterprises, Inc. a $500 million contract to build a new NASA facility for the Mars Project to be built in Lost River Texas—'cheap dirt and lots of it' is the rationale for choosing Lost River.

The town is projected to grow from a population of 10,000 to a mid-sized city of 250,000 within a scant three years as the Newton contractors and NASA employees move in. Big Ray envisions a bonanza of projects that he wants to develop, like strip malls and condominiums, townhouses, tennis courts, bars, and golf courses—all of this will spring up in the dry bottom lands of Texas which means that a dam will have to be built on the Lost River to store water, produce hydro power and irrigate new golf courses. There will be government contracts to build new water systems and treatment plants; more roads, more motels, bars, restaurants and fast food chains. Big Ray wants it all.

Lost River is also a perfect place for the new NRL league expansion race track and an ideal opportunity for Big Ray to build his dream; an entire community devoted to stock car racing. Bobby Wilson not only has a license for a race track in Lost River, but he actually registered three tracks—the dirt oval and go-cart tracks now in service plus a major concrete speedway for the future. And since the new law taxing tracks will only apply to new registrations, Bobby's licenses are grandfathered in and exempt.

But Bobby Wilson doesn't want to sell—especially to Big Ray Jones—and rejects Ray's offer to buy the track and licenses.

Race Day–Lap 140/300
Huntsville Raceland Speedway
Huntsville, Alabama

Jack Kelly alerts the audience that it is about time for a green flag pit stop and that the leaders will most likely will come in for fuel and tires within the next few laps. Larry Jenkins wonders when and who will come in? Tony Garland, now in the lead, approaches the pit road entrance and does a double fake, darting down, then up, then back down. At the last moment, he enters pit road. The fake out fails and Chapet, in second place, turns onto pit road right behind Tony with the field following suit.

RACE DAY IN ALABAMA

The reporter in Tony's pit shouts over the engine roar that there seems to be a problem with the jack. The jack man wrestles with it and finally gets it working. The right side tire changers get busy, but precious seconds have been lost. By the time the crew moves to the driver side, Chapet is out of his pit and leading the pack back on the track. Finally, Tony gets onto the track, but he has dropped to tenth place, right behind Bobby Jr. Tony is steaming mad and ignores his crew chief's radioed apology.

NRL Headquarters
Memphis, Tennessee
November, 2nd 2000

After Bobby Wilson turns down Big Ray's offer, Ray and Sam rethink their strategy and conclude they will have to go for a hostile takeover—not pursuing this opportunity would be a tragedy. Big Ray and Sam discuss the irony of the situation, how they both had always believed the NRL investigator's had covered for Bobby to avoid negative publicity and that Sam now has a chance to get even.

They make plans and Sam is tasked with reconnoitering the situation in Lost River. As usual, Sam will drive his van on the trip. Sam hates the way people look at him at airports and the indignity of how he was once treated by a flight attendant. And even though he could use the NRL corporate plane, Sam never does. Since being stuck in a wheelchair, Sam has become obsessed with controlling his means of transpiration and refused to rely upon others to get him around.

In essence, the van is Sam's corporate jet. It is not only designed for Sam to operate with hand controls, but it has a unique driver's side entry/ext ramp and quick wheel lock feature especially machined for his chair. With the van's heavily hot–rodded, big block turbocharged engine. race inspired suspension system, and custom designed mag wheels, the van will easily do 160 mph and can reach 60 mph in 3.5 seconds.

Sam plans to drive all night to avoid traffic, so he and Nancy enjoy an early dinner at a fancy steak house, she looking terrific in a low cut, black cocktail dress. They enjoy a bottle of French wine, then head home where Sam packs for the trip. He says he will call her every night, gets a deep kiss and heads out onto the freeway.

About twenty miles out of town he stops for a coffee and discovers that he has forgotten his brief case. He drives back to the NRL headquarters and uses his pass key to activate the freight elevator which takes him to the top floor. He rolls down the thickly carpeted hallway leading to his office and sees that the door to Big Ray's office at the end of corridor is slightly ajar and that there is a glimmer of light coming from inside. He wonders if Big Ray is still at work. He rolls closer to the door and hears heavy breathing and moans of passion. He smells perfume in the air and recognizes it as the same Nancy wore earlier in the evening. He peeks inside.

In the dim light he sees long, naked legs with an ankle bracelet with his race car number on it which he gave his wife ten years ago. He sees the black dress she had been wearing at dinner, draped on the end of the couch. The man making love to her is his friend and benefactor, Big Ray.

Sam retreats into his office, devastated and retrieves his briefcase and goes back down the elevator. He wonders how could she do it; how long has it been going on? As he pulls away in his van, he sees Nancy's silver SUV half hidden around the corner of the building.

The next four days in Lost River are hell for Sam. He thinks about Nancy constantly. He calls her after ten every night and gets the answering machine. When he finally connects with her in the afternoon, she explains that she has been going to bed early and shutting off the phone. His feelings of hurt are slowly replaced by anger at her and at Big Ray for playing him for a fool. His thoughts turn from his pain to revenge.

Race Day–Lap 160/300
Huntsville Raceland Speedway
Huntsville, Alabama

Jack Kelly reports that Tony, 'the Tornado,' is getting more and more frustrated in his effort to get around Bobby Jr. The rookie has managed to foil each of his attempts to pass. Both cars have been gaining position and are now running seventh and eighth with lap times matching Chapet who is still the race leader. Larry Jenkins points out that both cars show signs of swapping paint somewhere along the track.

The race show producer hands Kelly a note. Since the rookie has been doing so well, they decided to do some background research. It turns out that Tony and Junior have a history. They have not only competed in go karts and sprint cars, but they went to rival high schools. They don't seem to much like each other. Larry Jenkins wonders if this race is turning into a grudge match between two long-time adversaries.

NRL Headquarters
Memphis, Tennessee
November 3rd, 2004

This is their first face to face meeting since Sam returned from Lost River. Sam steels his resolve to hide his seething anger and tells Big Ray that, in spite of Bobby's business not being very successful, he has at least managed to keep his licenses current. However, he has fallen way behind on the bank loan that he took out to build the track and the bankers are pressing him to get current.

Bobby and his creditors are in the dark about the gold mine that he is sitting on. The situation looks ripe for a sneak attack. They decide that Big Ray will buy Bobby Wilson's outstanding note, call it in and foreclose on the property when Bobby can't come up with the cash. The Lost River Racetrack deal will come together by the end of the week.

Sam leaves a day in advance in his van in order to be at the San Antonio International Airport when Big Ray arrives in the NRL corporate jet. Leaving the airport they exit the freeway for the two lane road to Lost River. Big Ray pulls out a flask and offers it to Sam who declines. Halfway to Lost River, Sam pulls into a rest stop to take a break and Ray heads for the restroom. Sam uses his driver's side entry/exit ramp to make an inspection trip around the van, checking the tires. They load up and continue on towards Lost River.

Fifteen minutes later, the right front tire blows and Sam barely keeps the swerving van on the highway. Big Ray comments that Sam might have lost a little bit of his touch, but he concludes it was not too bad for someone now driving a desk for a living. They decide that because they are probably a good fifty miles from the nearest tow truck station, Ray should change the tire himself rather than waiting for AAA. Ray takes a swig from his flask then prepares to change the blown tire.

Big Ray tells Sam to turn up the music. Joking, Sam sticks his arm out the window and points to his wrist watch saying this is the longest pit stop in history and ordering Big Ray to change only one tire or they could get lapped. Ray throws the tire iron jack and dead tire into the back of the van. They continue on.

At the Community Bank of Lost River, Jeanette Parker, an old girl friend of Bobby's, phones him and tells him that she has just overheard her boss talking to Big Ray and that Ray is buying Bobby's note from the bank.

Bobby grabs his keys and rushes to the bank. He had expected a little more latitude, especially from a bank which he has patronized for twenty plus years, but now he remembers hearing a rumor that some of the bank's investments were in jeopardy because of the state's financial problems, so he fumes at himself for not paying more attention to the messages that the bank manager had been leaving on his answering machine.

Bobby pushes past the receptionist and shoves his way into the manager's office, just as Big Ray is signing the last page of the agreement. Bobby curses the manager and with fists balled lunges toward Big Ray. Quickly Sam swivels his wheel chair around and rolls in between Big Ray and Bobby then throws a hard punch into Bobby's stomach sending him reeling backwards. Falling back against the wall and gasping for air, Bobby's eyes focus on Sam and he says that he should have guessed that Sam would also be involved in going behind his back.

Alerted by the manager, the bank guard barges into the office, seizes Bobby from behind and rams him headfirst into the wall, then drags him out the door. The manager follows and grabs Bobby by his coat lapels and yells that he needs to either grow up or sober up. Then he tells the guard not to call the police, just make sure that Bobby is tossed. Back in his office he brings out a bottle of scotch, pours the booze into coffee mugs emblazoned with the bank logos and hands them to Big Ray and Sam. A toast to success is made.

RACE DAY IN ALABAMA

As usual around midnight, Bobby is in the town saloon, very drunk. Tonight he is complaining to anyone that will listen about how he is being ripped off by Big Ray and the bank. One of the regular bar girls takes pity on him and he and she cozy up, drink shots of Jack Daniels and dance to country tunes on the juke box. Bobby gives her his usual line about them getting married some day. She just smiles drunkenly.

Big Ray and Sam have just finished a lengthy conference call with the NRL accountant and attorney about the track deal and head for the only bar in town for a little celebration. Big Ray walks through the saloon doors, holding one open for Sam to wheel through, turns and through the smoke sees Bobby and the girl dancing. Sam makes a move to leave, but Ray grabs the grips on the back of the chair, saying that he wants to talk to Bobby to explain the situation, make him see reason, maybe even offer him a job. He clears a chair out of way at an empty table for Sam to roll into and heads to the bar to order drinks keeping an eye on Bobby in the mirror behind the bar. Bobby spots Big Ray in the mirror, shoves the girl away and charges Big Ray. They collide just as Big Ray is turning with two glasses of whiskey and ice. Both men end up half over the bar, Big Ray bent backwards and soaked by the drinks.

Two burly security young men wearing orange nylon jackets with the word 'Security' in bold print on the back grab and march both Big Ray and Bobby out the back door of the bar into the alley with the admonition to settle it out here or don't come back.

This draws a small audience of bar regulars that file outside to see the action. Big Ray and Bobby slug it out in the alley. Big Ray finally knocks Bobby out and the bar girl screams at him that he didn't have to hurt Bobby that bad. When Big Ray comes back into the bar after the fight he is pretty beat up, over excited and angry. Still he brags to the bartender and some of the patrons that it was a hell of a fight, Texas style i.e. anything goes, but he finally kicked Bobby's butt. He said that Bobby had insulted him, fought dirty and that Bobby was damn lucky that he didn't kill him. Big Ray says that if the two ever mix it up again, that it might just happen. He pretends not to see Bobby collapsed at a table at the back of the room with the girl dabbing at his head with a wet bar towel. Big Ray and Sam slug down their drinks then head back to the motel next door.

At seven the next morning, the sheriff, notified by a local homeless person, finds Bobby dead in the alley, his head smashed in. A tire iron is found in a garbage can near the crime scene. Lab tests discover Bobby's blood and Big Ray's prints on the tire iron. DNA tests finger Big Ray. The time of death is estimated to be between two AM and four AM.

Since there are two reports of Big Ray scuffling with Bobby the day before, one at the bank and one at the bar after which the bartender claims that Big Ray threatened to kill Bobby.

Big Ray is brought in for questioning. Big Ray admits to fighting Bobby but denies killing him. Big Ray says that of course he recognizes the tire iron, he used it to change a flat tire on Sam's van. But when the Sheriff checks the van parked in the motel next to the bar, he finds a perfectly good spare tire and tire iron. The young kid serving as the photographer for the local newspaper has a field day shooting digital stills of the van's interior and exterior. This is the first murder that he has ever covered.

Big Ray is booked for murder. The trial is set to take place in six months and he is in jail, denied bail. Ray's lawyer urges him to stretch out the process because as things stand now, he has no defense, no alibi, and little chance of being acquitted. Ray insists that he is being framed.

Bobby's funeral at the Lost River racetrack brings out the fans, local racers, neighbors, drunks that knew Bobby from the bar, and a few curious onlookers. The ceremony is short and to the point. Kate and Bobby Jr ride in the back of pickup truck slowly dribbling out Bobby's ashes as they tour around the track. Then for a wild and tumultuous fifteen minutes, dozens of hot cars spin doughnuts and burn rubber in tribute to Bobby. Slowly the spectators drift out the gate, leaving Kate and Junior holding onto one another in the dusk. Jay sits alone, watching them from the bleachers.

Race Day—Lap 220/300
Huntsville Raceland Speedway
Huntsville, Alabama

Jack Kelly announces that Tony Garland finally gets by Junior and that this could be a close race for second and third, but that Chapet was now over five seconds in the lead. Larry Jensen speculates that now that Tony and Jr. have fallen into line that they could catch up with Chapet in ten or so laps if the course stays green, or sooner if the yellow flag comes out.

Lost River Jail
Lost River Texas
Three Weeks Ago

Ray continues to insist that he is innocent. No one is listening, except Kate who originally came to the jail to ask Big Ray why he had to kill her father if Big Ray thought he was going to get the track anyway. She then tells him that the contract has been voided by the bank due to false representation. He can fight it if he wants, but she has taken out a personal loan and has paid the bank the past due amount. She also explains that in Texas, there is a provision for either party of a contract to void it within a twenty-four hour period unless specifically stated otherwise in the agreement. She adds that maybe the NRL lawyers in Tennessee didn't know that because there was no exclusion clause in the note assumption contract.

Big Ray's response is to offer Kate a job defending him just in case his Tennessee lawyers have missed something else, like the fact that he didn't murder her father. Over the next week Kate thinks it over. Jay Garland is only too willing to help Why would Big Ray kill her father? Drunken rage? Revenge? If he really was the killer, what was his motive?

RACE DAY IN ALABAMA

But, if Big Ray was innocent as he claims, how did the missing wheel and flat tire figure into the case?

Jay tells Kate that he recalls that the mag wheels on Sam's van differed from any he had seen before and might be an original design. He explains how a high tech, computer-controlled machine tool can sculpt metal like butter. They locate the reporter who gives them a copy of the photos he took in Sam's van on a floppy disk. In Jay's shop office, they use a photo enhancement program to blow a closeup of the wheel and find a tiny etching, 'Wheels of Fire.' They check the web and find that the company is located in Memphis.

Jay pretends to be a deputy sheriff from Lost River and calls the wheel fabricator. The owner says to FAX a photo of the wheel to him. Jay complies. The owner calls back and identifies the wheel and tells him that a set of five was originally made for Sam Strong, but he had also ordered another one about two months ago: he didn't say why he needed it.

Kate and Jay reason that Sam must have been planning the murder for some time, stashing a new wheel and tire beforehand to replace the blowout in the van and then disposing of the flat tire and wheel some-where the same night. Somehow he must have rigged the tire to fail on the trip to Lost River with Big Ray. Sam would have known that Bobby Wilson would be at the bar. After all it was common knowledge that he was there pretty much every night. And getting Big Ray to the bar for a drink would not have been that hard to arrange.

Lost River is a small town, one bar, one motel, and one dump, so they reason that they should be able to find the evidence: the mag wheel and flat tire. Sam would certainly not risk having them in his possession so he must have gotten rid of them that night. They begin a search for the blown tire with a custom made wheel.

They start at the gas station next to the motel where Big Ray and Sam stayed the night of the murder. They find a pile of old tires and even a rusty tire iron in the back near the alley but nothing matching the items that they are looking for.

Kate and Jay are sitting in the deserted bleachers at the track when Kate suggests that maybe they are looking at the problem backwards. If Sam is the murderer, he needed not only to get rid of the old wheel and tire, but replace them with a new set before the van was inspected. Big Ray was sure that there was only one spare tire in the van, not two. So Sam only had about a two hour window to commit the murder, hide the old wheel and flat tire and replace it with the new set.

So where did the other wheel and tire come from? Jay suggests that they should check out the storage locker firm at the east end of town. The redneck manager is not particularly helpful. He comments that business is bad. The only handicapped person he has seen in the area was the dude in a wheelchair that was interested in buying the company but he didn't rent any lockers, just looked the place over.

RACE DAY IN ALABAMA

The manager says he and his and wife were seriously considering accepting the offer until it was withdrawn. Kate asks the manager if he recalls which lockers the man inspected. He replies that about half of the lockers on the backside are empty but he doesn't remember which ones the guy looked at. The manager recalls that he told the gent to have a look on his own, but that didn't apply to them unless they have a search warrant. The manager says he recognizes Kate and doesn't want to get mixed up in her father's murder or whatever they are up to.

Back at the track office, Kate and Jay figure that since it is now common knowledge that Sam, Ray and the NRL were trying to put together a deal to develop Lost Falls, they probably wanted to buy the storage locker property for some project, maybe even to keep it as a business. She doubts that they will be able to get a search warrant, especially since the mayor and her father never got along.

The mayor still gripes that ever since the Wilson's came back to Lost River, there has been trouble in this usually peaceful, sleepy little town. His constituents, especially the ones that don't fancy car racing, complain that the town's reputation has been tarnished by the murder. So without official police oversight, Kate and Jay will have to check out the lockers on the QT.

That night they meet back at the track wearing gloves and dark clothing and joke about starting their own detective agency and spying on cheating spouses and solving jewelry robberies. They park Jay's pickup about a half mile away from the storage business. The single light on a pole out front reveals that there are no cars in the parking lot.

Kate and Jay walk around to the back where they find about three dozen large lockers. They roll up the doors of each of the unlocked units and find that they are all empty. Kate points out the different brands of locks securing the occupied units and figures that it is likely that the renters furnish their own locks. Jay points out that most of the locks are old and rusty, but there are three shiny, new looking ones.

Jay tells Kate to wait, there is something in the truck he needs. When he returns, he is carrying a set of bolt cutters. The first lock they cut secures a locker jammed with furniture. The next one is packed floor to ceiling with cardboard boxes filled with religious fliers and pornographic magazines. A worn-looking life-size, inflatable love doll stands guard over the bizarre collection.

Kate and Jay move to the final unit. Kate crosses her fingers as Jay cuts the lock. Their flashlight picks out the mag wheel and flat tire leaning against the back wall of the unit. Jay rolls the tire away from the wall and points out that this is a top-rated high-speed tire, and shows Kate that the tread and the sidewalls are like new. On the rim, Jay points out the signature from the manufacturer, 'Wheels of Fire.'

RACE DAY IN ALABAMA

Kate discovers a plastic bag on the floor. She opens it and a small shiny, metal object falls into her hand. Jay explains that it is a special wrench used to adjust the valve core inside the valve stem of the tire.

He checks the core with the wrench. Normally it should be screwed in tightly to hold in the air, but this one is slightly loose. Air would slowly leak out. He figures that only a smart car-guy like Sam would have thought up this scheme of starting a slow leak to cause a tire failure. Obviously the flat tire was an excuse to get Big Ray's fingerprints on the tire iron and rim. Kate observes that this was a well planned, premeditated murder.

Now they are convinced that Sam is the murderer, but Kate says the evidence is inadmissible because they did not have a court issued search warrant. They decide that they need to confront Sam directly with the evidence and make him confess to the crime. Jay puts the little valve wrench back into the plastic bag and totes the wheel and tire back to the truck.

They wake up Bobby Jr, load up Jay's pickup and head out for Memphis. Bobby Jr can't help but notice that Kate is sitting close to Jay.

Race Day—Lap 280/300
Huntsville Raceland Speedway
Huntsville, Alabama

Jack Kelly comments that once again the yellow flag is out due to a big crash on turn four involving five or six cars. Larry Jensen says that this is exactly what Chapet didn't want. All of drivers on the lead lap stream down pit road, Chapet, Garland, and Junior followed by the rest of the pack. Jack offers that with only twenty laps to go, fuel is not an issue, so will they take two or four tires? Larry says he would take a full set for better grip at this stage in the race, which is exactly what Chapet and Garland do, but Junior only takes two on the right side and leaves pit row as the race leader. As Junior roars by, Tony yells at his crew chief to do something...he just shrugs his shoulders.

Memphis, Tennessee
Two Weeks Ago

After dropping Bobby Jr at the Memphis Speedway track to hobnob with racers and mechanics, Kate and Jay meet Nancy Strong at a small café not far from NRL headquarters. She says that ever since Sam returned from Lost River he has been a different man. She wants a divorce but is afraid to ask because Sam has become physically abusive and now she fears for her life. She adds that she thinks Sam is going crazy and blames herself for causing him so much pain. She looks pretty beat up with a black eye. Kate tells her that they think Sam is the murderer, not Big Ray.

Nancy breaks down and tell them of her affair with Big Ray. The murder motive gets stronger. Nancy agrees to help put Sam in jail. They go to the Memphis police for help. Even though Nancy confesses that she and Big Ray are lovers, the cops are convinced that she is telling the truth and agree to help. They sign onto a plan to smoke out Sam hatched by Kate and Jay,

Sam, sitting behind Big Ray's desk looks through the stack of mail awaiting his attention and picks up the large envelope marked 'URGENT' in bright red ink. Opening it he finds two color 8 x 10 photographs of his custom mag wheel and the flat tire. On back of one of the pictures is a handwritten note, 'Flat, 'Wheels of Fire' brand tire with a leaky valve-stem core for sale at the bargain price of $100,000 in one hundred dollar bills. If interested, bring the money to the silver Winnebago parked next to the Werner Dodge team garage at the speedway at 5 PM."

The Memphis cops rig Kate with a wire. Bobby Jr, Kate, Jay, Nancy and a Memphis police detective hide in the Winnebago. Right on time, Sam pulls up in his high-powered van. The mechanics working on the cars in the Werner garage barely notice.

Sam parks the van next to the silver RV and taps his horn. He holds a brief case up to the windshield. The door of the motor home opens and Kate steps out. Surprised, Sam wants to know what she is doing here. She reaches down and tugs off a tarp covering the tire and wheel. Then she holds up the plastic bag with the valve-stem wrench.

Sam realizes that he is in serious trouble. Panicked, he fumbles under the dash and retrieves a 45 caliber Colt pistol which he aims at Kate. He tells her if she wants to live, she had better roll the wheel up the ramp into the back of the van. He activates the rear ramp and swivels so that he can keep her in his sights.

Kate does as he orders and asks Sam if he killed her father. Sam shouts that he did and that he waited for him in the alley until the bar closed. He knew Bobby always went out the back door to avoid being arrested for being drunk in public. He says that Bobby stumbled in a pothole and was on his knees throwing up so it was easy to roll over and slam him over the head. He tells her that her father had put him in a wheelchair for life and this was just a case of justice being served.

Waiving the pistol, Sam motions for Kate to get in the passenger seat. She asks why, he says do it or that he will shoot her right here and right now. He swivels his chair and locks it back in place, the rear ramp quickly stows and locks in place. He puts the van in reverse, then heads back to the speedway entrance.

Jay, Bobby Jr, Nancy and the detective pile out of the RV. The officer radios a police cruiser to close in and seal the track. The Memphis sheriff's sedan lumbers ahead and just barely manages to block the escape route. Sam slides to a stop, spins his wheels in reverse, then heads down the access road toward the south exit. Another cruiser moves into place blocking the way. Sam changes course again, heads over the grass apron onto the concrete speedway track and quickly picks up speed.

Jay points Bobby Jr towards one of the Werner race cars being prepared for testing. Junior grabs a helmet while Jay rounds up a fuel canister and tops off the tank.

The Werner master mechanic, Johnny 'Crashwall' Dobbs asks them what's up and Bobby Jr blurts out that he has to save his sister. Crashwall helps Junior strap in while the detective calls for more backup.

Suddenly the garage comes to life with the roar of an 800 horsepower engine. Bobby Jr peels out and blasts onto the access road at the top of the tri-oval. He sees Sam's van on the opposite side of the track and remembers that the tires are cold and that this is the hottest car that he has ever driven. He has no real plan except somehow to try to rescue his sister.

In the van, Sam is raging on about how he framed Ray because he has been having sex with his slut of a wife. Kate decides to attack. She reaches across and tries to grab the pistol sitting in his lap. Sam's legs are useless, but his upper body is in superb condition. He takes his right hand off the wheel, backhands her hard flinging her into her seat while the van swerves nearly out of control. Sam retrieves the pistol and aims it at her forehead. Seeing the wild look in his face and staring down the barrel of his gun, she decides to cool it and buckles her shoulder harness.

In the rear view mirror Sam sees a stock car gaining fast. Farther behind there is a covey of blue flashing lights trailing into the distance. Sam slows a bit to size up his pursuer letting him come up along the passenger side. He curses when he realizes that it is Bobby Jr.

Sam drives hard into the corner then jerks the steering wheel left and right making the rear end fish-tail—as if the van was about to break loose and the vehicle was way out of its league on a race track. As he slows, Sam gradually drops lower on the track and just as Junior noses up on the high side, Sam wrenches the wheel hard right pinning Bobby Jr against the wall and holding him there. The wall grinds through the side of Junior's car. Sparks of hot metal and smoke fill the inside. Sam is so crazed at this point that he is having flashbacks from earlier races. He is hearing messages from his spotter telling him to stay high and pin the other driver against the wall. His fantasy pit boss is telling him only one more lap and the NRL championship is his.

As they move through turn four, the pressure exerted by the van relaxes for a moment and Bobby Jr. hits the brakes. The van shoots forward and away. Two police cruisers zoom by Junior, lights flashing and sirens screaming. Now clear of the wall and the van, Bobby Jr mashes the accelerator. The wild car chase continues.

Junior catches up with and passes the two Memphis Police cruisers like they were standing still. The van is just ahead with a blossoming plume of tire smoke coming from its right side. Bobby Jr stays away from the dangerous dead man's zone between the van and the wall. Going into the next turn, Bobby Jr. follows just behind the van, then drifts up to the top of the track to gain momentum, then abruptly angles down to the bottom where he carefully taps the left rear bumper of Sam's van causing it to spin out and crash head-on into the wall. Inside the van, the heavy wheel and flat tire that Kate had stored bounces around and slams into the back of Sam's head, stunning him. Bobby Jr hits the brakes and skids to a stop. He reverses the car, and backs toward Sam's van. He jams the rear of the race car against the driver's door, trapping Sam inside.

Junior jumps out and rushes to the passenger side. There is smoke streaming from the van. He sees Kate struggling to get out, but the door is wedged shut. Sam comes to and tries to restart the engine. An NRL emergency vehicle arrives and parks next to the wreck. Crashwall and Jay pile out along with two paramedics. Kate is struggling against the door and screaming for help. Crashwall grabs a set of the jaws of life carried by one of the paramedics and within seconds the door is popped, a cloud of smoke blooms out and Kate is freed. She waives off the paramedics, saying that she is OK.

Sam is coughing and struggling to free himself from his custom driver control station. Blocked by Bobby Jr's car, the ramp on the driver's side won't lower locking his chair in place. Crashwall reaches in from the passenger side, frees Sam from his harness and roughly pulls him clear of his chair across the van and onto the ground. The paramedics pick Sam up and place him on a stretcher then roar out in a rush of flashing lights and sirens. Crashwall orders everyone back to a safe distance away from the van. He looks down. Ironically the chase has ended at the track's finish line.

Kate turns to Jay and tells him thanks for saving her. She holds her head up and Jay kisses her. He makes a comment that he hopes it won't take so much adventure to get the next kiss. Kate jabs him in the ribs

Flames start to lick the outside of the van. Everyone backs away, but Junior dives into the stock car, fires it up and screeches away in reverse just as the van violently explodes. Junior exits the car and spots Bob Werner, owner of the Werner Racing Enterprises, shaking his head while surveying his battered race car. Bobby Jr mouths the words, "Uh-Oh!"

Werner compliments Bobby Jr on his bump and run move and says that the NRL cameras taped the entire episode and that it should be in the highlight films for years. He explains that they are trying to build a race team for the future based upon new drivers working their way up through the divisions and that they just happen to be short a driver due to his having an emergency appendectomy. Werner asks if Junior might like to test this week in Huntsville in order to qualify for the last race in Alabama. Junior nods and shakes his hand. Werner laughs.

Race Day–Lap 297/300
Huntsville Raceland Speedway
Huntsville, Alabama

RACE DAY IN ALABAMA

Jack Kelly reports that this is one of the best races ever broadcast on television. Chapet takes the high line and barely edges past Junior but there is traffic ahead. Tony is right on Bobby Jr's rear bumper, pushing from behind. Junior's spotter directs him to move up behind Chapet, they are about to lap a car who will move down and out of way. In a flash they are past the lapped car and Tony has to let off the gas to avoid rear-ending the lapped car. His spotter is getting an awful earful of rage.

Race Day–Final Lap 299/300
Huntsville Raceland Speedway
Huntsville, Alabama

Tony catches the new leaders as they duel side by side and Junior finds himself the meat in a stock car sandwich. Tony smashes Junior in the right quarter panel, pushing him up into Chapet, a lucky move for Junior because it bounces him off Chapet and keeps him from spinning out. They are three abreast coming down the straightaway, Tony is on the bottom jerking his wheel to the right bumping Junior and Chapet is on top jerking his wheel to the left to keep Junior from pushing him into the wall. The crowd is on its feet, cheering madly. They cross the finish line in a dead heat. NRL officials huddle at a monitor displaying the three-way photo finish. The network replays it over and over again while the crowd roars on its feet.

Over the PA system, the track announcer is heard to whisper and ask are you sure? Then he booms the message, "You fans have just witnessed one of the closest finishes in NRL history. Less than 5/100th of a second separate the top three finishers. The race winner is Bobby Wilson, Jr. in his first ever NRL race. Second is Jim Chapet, and the new NRL champion, Third is Tony 'the Tornado' Garland runner up in the championship." The crowd goes wild.

Big Ray and Nancy assume a prominent place in the winner's circle. Hugs and congratulations are exchanged as Junior, Chapet and Garland take their spots on the victory stand and do their bows and spray the crowd with champagne.

After the announcers, reporters and cameras disperse, Tony comes over to Jay and sticks out his hand in a friendly gesture. Junior reaches for Tony's hand. With a tight lipped smile, Tony delivers an upper cut to Bobby Jr's chin lifting him off the ground landing him on his butt. Junior rubs his chin and then grins. He figures that this is Tony's tough way of welcoming the rookie to the big league and that the battle between them is just beginning. Big Ray laughs uproariously. Kate smacks Big Ray in the head with her water bottle. This ignites a scuffle and the drivers, mechanics and owners join in the ruckus and mayhem.

Jack Kelly says that this was the most thrilling stock car race in history. Larry Jenkins agrees and adds that the good news is that they only have to wait six months until the next one.

The End
Edited by Michael H.D. Dormer

LONGEVITY GENE

Year 2029
BioGenetics International (BGI)
Berkeley, California

D r. Astra Sturtevant, a head-turning Brazilian girl in her mid-twenties was not only beautiful but also brilliant...and in big trouble! She was just concluding the third year of her postdoc in advanced longevity research at BioGenetics International and so far she was shooting blanks in terms of positive results.

The foremost researchers from universities around the world came to BGI to investigate, probe and manipulate the fundamental elements of living systems. As long as they were productive and young, which the lab director narrow mindedly believed to be one and the same, they were welcome.

But as soon as they lost their edge, or they reached the grand old age of thirty, they were discarded like last year's model hover car. Nevertheless, still running fine and with good blades on them, they were shipped off to make room for the next fleet of brilliant, young scientists charged with new energy and new ideas

According to the standard measure used to rate

scientific institutions, i.e. papers cited in the technical literature, the strategy was a resounding success. The lab had produced more than its share of biomedical breakthroughs and had generated lots of royalties for BGI...and a hefty number of burned out minds as well.

In the mid-morning light, the modern research laboratory in the center of the BGI campus seemed to fade and emerge as waves of fog rolled in from across the bay. The fog provided a bit of relief from the blistering heat when it momentarily blocked the sun. In spite of the two decade drought and strict water rationing, a fountain at the entryway ostentatiously gushed water into the air attracting flocks of thirsty pigeons and kids wading in the pool.

By the time Astra reached her office on the third floor, preferring to walk instead of taking the elevator, she was dripping with sweat. But like most modern day women working in the sweltering Bay Area these days, she kept a backup blouse and slacks ready for a quick change.

Now wearing fresh clothes, she slid into a lightweight, plastic lab coat with 'Dr. Sturtevant' embroidered above the BGI emblem, snapped on the mandatory surgical gloves and bio-filter mask and then unlocked the door of her small, private lab.

Depending upon a researcher's chosen field of study, a molecular biology lab might house rhesus monkeys, cell cultures, or even a collection of plants. Astra's lab was unique in that it contained dozens of aquariums each providing a home for hundreds of very small, freshwater flatworms known scientifically as *Planaria*.

Astra's line of flatworms were tiny critters about a half inch long and an eighth of an inch wide. Although they had no real commercial value, *Planaria* remained a mystery to science. If they were cut in half, the head end would regenerate a new tail. But if they were sliced in two lengthwise down the middle; each half would develop into a separate living worm, thus generating a new pair of flatworms. That might be of interest to scientists studying tissue regeneration, but the current research thrust at BGI was the aging process in higher level organisms—not simple flatworms as the director was fond of reminding her.

Scientists had known for years that a culture of human stem cells would flourish in a culture dish as long as nutrients were provided. They would grow and divide time after time, but after a certain number of cell divisions they would suddenly stop reproducing and perish. Billions of research dollars later, all that was known was that something turned off the gene that instructed the DNA of the stem cells to replicate. One theory that had gained a certain degree of popularity conjectured that a genetic clock was somehow embedded into the DNA code.

The foundation of Astra's studies began back in the 1960s when a zoologist from the University of Kansas published an obscure paper which was soon buried in the literature with little recognition at the time by the scientific community. He had found, and Astra always wondered why anyone would ever have thought of such a novel experiment, that if he alternately starved and fed a certain species of *Planaria*, it would live for decades—normally that particular species had a lifespan three years or less.

And like back then, no one at BGI today regarded the flatworm rejuvenation phenomenon to be anything more than a mere curiosity...except Astra who seemed to have the entire field to herself—at least no one else had published any follow-up studies in recent years.

Experiments spanning decades were rarely conducted and Astra often wondered how the KU zoologist had the persistence to monitor his experiments for twenty-plus years.

Astra couldn't conceive of waiting that long for her results so she used a genetically modified *Planaria* that had a limited lifespan of only two weeks due to a mutation that she had induced that restricted their ability to synthesize telomerase, an enzyme that protects chromosomes when they replicate. She reasoned that if she could identify and manipulate the mutated worms' genetic clock to increase their lifespans to four weeks, she would be able to claim a one hundred percent increase in longevity—but so far the experiments had been a dismal failure.

Although ostensibly part of the BGI Gerontology Research Group, the offbeat nature of her work had not endeared her to the lab director. Now in her third year of wheel spinning, even she was beginning to wonder if she might have chosen the wrong subject to investigate. It looked more and more like a dead end and the way Director Horowitz treated her, she had begun to doubt that her contract would be renewed for another year.

Horowitz had seemed skeptical from the outset that Astra's work with *Planaria* might meaningfully contribute to the development of commercial longevity enhancing drugs for the burgeoning pharmaceutical market, but Astra's grant from the World Institute of Health had opened the door at BGI. And since her work did involve the study of aging, Horowitz had begrudgingly accepted Astra's appointment to the lab. Astra's research certainly lacked the luster of other aging related projects at BGI and she found herself increasingly on her own with little interchange or opportunity for collaboration with other scientists.

There were plenty of other organisms that had lengthy lifespans. Bristle cone pines in the California desert had been dated at well over three thousand years of age so her research on a twenty-year-old flatworm wasn't nearly as glamorous as compared to the work of Horowitz's showcase of postdoctoral prima donnas which was focused on systematically refining the map of the human genetic code and determining which genes might regulate the aging process.

Since experimenting on humans was currently illegal, the research at BioGenetics International was only theoretical and intended to provide a foundation for gene manipulation that might occur decades in the future. Still the possibility of prolonging the human lifespan was currently the hot topic for commercial drug companies and medical practitioners. Understandably Horowitz was taking full advantage of the opportunity to secure as much funding for as many new research projects as possible.

The termination of Astra's appointment at BGI would mean that she could no longer put off joining her father's herbal products company back in Brazil and she would have wasted three precious years of grant funding, which would likely taint her chances for financial support down the road. It would definitely be a major blow to her career.

Astra activated her notepad and prayed that she would finally make a breakthrough. Suddenly the lab lights flickered out and then snapped back on just as a tremendous clap of thunder reverberated throughout downtown Berkeley's forest of skyscrapers.

Astra looked out the window and was happy to see a sprinkling of raindrops on the glass. Tropical squalls like this were quite rare in the Bay Area and never lasted long, but Astra was from Brazil and dearly loved the rain. Even though most of the precipitation evaporated before it hit the ground, she thought of the brief downpour as an omen of good things to come. She laughed and said, *"World get ready...my worms and I are coming to set you free!"*

****

Longevity Gene is from Chapter One of Met-Chron Sanctuary which is the first novel in the Metamorphosis Chronicles series. It and the rest of the series are available at www. planetropolis.com

One Hundred Crows

Floating with the wind as it struck the
cliff and roared upward, providing the
flock of crows with a break from gravity
and a free ride across the sky.

One hundred crows wheeled and
swung, dove and climbed in unison as
each of the young males waited impa-
tiently for his chance for a few seconds
in which he would lead the flock and
the others would instinctively follow.

After that, he knew that he had to re-
linquish command as his rivals waited
for their turn at the helm of the flock.

Dance of the Seagulls

Seagulls dancing in the wind.
If only we could read their thoughts,
we would hear them laughing and
singing in the sunset light.

But, they know they must be heading
home...out of the new rain sliding down.

But, they say....
Just one more circle.
One more turn.
One more pass over the big tree.

Then back to the beach sand to wait for
dawn...to do it all over again.

Dark Shark

On Dark Shark—sensuous omni-whore
of the down there.
Come from the nothingness of lonely flu-
id
   and slip nearer each orbit.
Closer—then to dynamite away, then...
   once again, The Orbit.
She tosses—flashes the beauty of her
steel
    flesh, perfect in form...waiting to
touch.
The Scorpio Lady of Death—she Orbits.

Each time again and again, she the lusty
   fox caressed by her universe mother.
Circling closer, nearer and nearer—
   tightening the Orbit!

Now I know that she my life must de-
cide,
   and still closer the Orbit.

Wait... Where...?

 Spin around, she is nowhere!
   Gone?
No too late!

From below the Master comes
   and takes.

Full come the Orbit!

Swim Free

Swim free Noble Sea Chiefs, twist and turn on your gliding way through water space.

Pirouette again and again, taste the freedom of the sea. And chant...
"No man creature can reach us, we the Noble Sea Chiefs."

Find clear water, find reefs free of man. Twist and turn and glide in ecstasy.
"Let us alone," the Sea Chiefs cry..."Let us be free."

"No man creature can reach us...we the Noble Sea Chiefs."

Even so far beneath the clouds, the Sea Chiefs feel the warmth of the limitless summer sun. Their water space snaps in blue sparkles. The Sea Chiefs pivot around Silver Leader; oscillating in perfect formation. They chant together..."No man creature can reach us, we the Noble Sea Chiefs."

The Sea Chiefs go down past secret moats to their castle in the sea.
The Chiefs circle and look cautiously behind. No one must follow. No one must see. The Sea Chiefs end patrol and rejoin their families. They whisper..."No man creature can reach us; we the Noble Sea Chiefs.

The Starlet

I thought I was too old for love.
Because most days
   had lost their brilliance.
The taste of wine not so new, a beer but
another brew.

But then, a new spark—a breath of
billowy clouds in the sky.
A new lady, much younger than I.
She just in her beginning. with days
fresh from her first breath of air and each
breath always one to remember.

A touch, her small hand against mine.
She caring.
Me the one always plunging into endless
worlds of frustration.
Wanting to give, but only to find despair.
Caressing, and sweating away the energy
of creativity writing words like these.
All forgotten in the moment of a single
touch.

She, the Young One. Me the Strong.
She the Fox. Me the Stag.
She the Inspiration. Me the Bull.
She the Starlet. Me the Wisher.

Honolulu Crazies

Its found in the weaving through Hotel
Street perversions, green light, red
light, stop and go conversions.

Tranquil island paradise filled with
General Motors strife...

A gentle Polynesian stock driven mad by
Toyota shock.

Mercedes–Bug, Porsche–Ford,
  Primo, Kirin, Oly horde.

Chevron, Union, Exxon fill
  the air with hydrocarbons for me to
swill.

Matson Lines deliver one more
regurgitation–all in need of license
registration.

In quiet country solace, it occurs to
me...

  How can this be?

RON S. NOLAN

Soaring Again

Oh the anticipation—surging plummets, and maybe 'up' that goes 'boost' bending wings and tugging hard against the harness.

Once again, after so many wasted thermals, the 'twang' of tautness in the wings as they pulse and release.

Gently turn to the right, lift to weightlessness to then sink in sync, and then back again,. Oh...she goes up hard!

More coolness near the billowy white cloud base, then to continue to soar upward and then disappear into the fragile mist.

Once again to suddenly re-awake as our punch scores the furled brow—up to the eye, then down past the beard and up and over and then out to clear air.

Faster, higher—

Out again—on top, roll to a look down and see running horses struggling to pull a Conestoga: jostling the miracle fish drowsing in reflective pools.

All the above encompassed in the cloud's personality imagery that stimulates the imagination!

Once again, the strong, binding force that twists my mind towards home.

Once again down, down.

Back, back down to the Earth again.

Lightning flashes, thunder rolls

and it begins to rain.

Soaring with Pelicans

Now I chase the clouds, soar with
pelicans along the sea.

Not to get away, but just to go.

Not to leave the Earth, but to see it from
above.

The things that I cherished most before
were only ways out of my mind.

The things that I cherish now are so few
—yet they are so real that I will never
forget.

The Wreck of the Liki Liki

We have come to remember the wreck of the Liki Liki. She lies upon the reef down below. Her stack is exposed, but nobody knows what treasure lies beneath her coal.

The Liki Liki was a trader.
She sailed the tropical seas.
Never in Bristol fashion, her cargo always rationed.

On the final cruise, the Liki's cargo was black coal she brought from 'Hono' in her hold. The coal was fuel for the onshore train, but she had brought it in vain. Mahukona would be her final goal.

She tried to cross the Alenuihaha on a day the channel seas were high. The Captain did his best, but never the less, the poor ship was soon bound to die.

They threw her ground tackle about her after she had run up on the reef. No one realized her plight, as they worked through the night.

The Liki Liki went down that day—never to sail the seas again. Still her name resounds in local lore. The Liki Liki had finally found her end.

Field of Flowers

The lush field above the bay has once again been reborn.
Like when the Sokel tribe lived here in a time long ago and the dried tules of their huts flapped in the sea breeze.
Missionaries no longer forcing them to their knees.
Crows, swallows and gulls fly overhead above the green grass with waves like those in the sea below.
A place of beauty and power...
Yet once again, they will soon murder the grass and flowers in the field for reasons that they will only know.

The Fly

I found a fly in the bathroom.
I chased him out with my broom.
But at the last minute, he came about.
"I am not a guy," screamed the fly.
And bit me on the ear so hard I had to cry.

Momentum

Morning wake up and you feel it burn-
ing, churning inside, but just lie there.

Don't rush it. Let it surface—find its own
way through the civilization confusion.

Its not just another day; the sounds,
smells and early morning colors are
alive, bursting with a secret that only
you knew in the night.

Gently drift, let the energy flow. More
clarity and the focus resolves...and then
you see it! The sun...the source.

A day of meaning...a day of moving. A
dawn that promises creativity. The yel-
low radiance of the sun warms your
limbs and your mind.

Time to rise. Time to do.

Poet/Artist Breaks the Rules

Roll, rubble, tumble, jumble
freedom to be free......———.......
Brind, gessusch, gading, gagi
structure?....That's not for me.

To do as expected is not to be free...
shananzel, garbunzel, quanastal, kabee.

To do as expected is not for me.
Mabu, Kuba, Zaining, Smozee.

'Tis the call of the...
lecherous life apprenticee!

ABOUT THE AUTHOR

Ron S. Nolan, Ph.D. lives in Aptos, California near the sunken ship at the end of the pier in SeaCliff Beach. He spends his days working out, running, writing and performing tech patent research–quite a leap from his early days in Western Kansas where he shared the farm outhouse with a nest of half frozen rattlesnakes and learned to read by the light of a Coleman lantern! To learn more about his latest novels and screenplays, please visit...

Planetropolis Publishing
www.planetropolis.com

****

An engaging adventure about
a pair of paranormal dolphins!

Preview

eBook and Paperback versions
are available at www.planetropolis.com

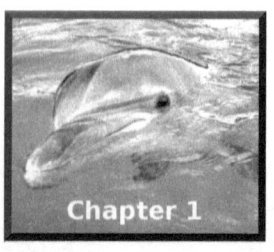

Chapter 1

Key West, Florida 1965

Newcomers to Key West–at least those who came in search of island history, often as not received directions to the order of, "It's near the center of the grounds...just look for the birds. You'll find it." And looking up they would seem to notice for the first time the gaggles of gulls circling and screaming–a kind of parody of nearby Duval street along which shuttled disoriented tourists in a never ending, back and forth, coast to coast rush. Homing in towards the center of attraction, the visitors would find a full-sized, steam-powered locomotive, a relic of Averell Harriman's inter-island railroad, standing rock-solid on a short section of track, baking waves of searing heat from its shiny black plate. Seagulls perpetually slid and crisscrossed over-head, sometimes landing briefly before lifting off towards the crystalline sand of Baker Beach and the rich fishing grounds of the Gulf. The train served as a social commons for the birds; a strutting ground where newly formed pairs enacted their preprogrammed rituals of courtship–leaving beneath their perches frozen drips, like vanilla frosting melting in the hot sun. Small well-kept clapboard houses crafted in the classic style of historic Key West bordered Mac Arthur Park. Like most of the homes in the neighborhood, the Grant residence was washed chalk-white. The front porch was screened as protection against Florida's ravenous mosquitoes and remained cool even in the heat of the afternoon.

Overhead, suspended by brass links, a carved wooden sign in bright paint announced 'GRANT'S PET SHOP.' A green and red enameled parrot grasped the top of the 'O' in the word 'SHOP' hanging tight with yellow talons. A busy jungle of tropical banana, pink and red bougainvillea, and blazing birds of paradise engulfed the small yard separated from the sidewalk by a cedar hedge. Cement birdbaths and low benches were stashed haphazardly in the lush foliage. Looking more like a home than a business, a passerby would have never guessed the extent of the menagerie within–especially in the middle of a very quiet neighborhood in Key West, Florida during the summer of 1965.

Past the porch packed with faded wicker furniture and choked waist-high with neat stacks of yellowed newspapers, a wooden door with a cracked white porce-lain knob led into the shop proper. Assorted bamboo birdcages, small and large, jammed side-by-side, harbored chirping, and flitting, tropical birds in efful-gent plumage. A chorus of demanding mynas, punctu-ated by piercing monkey screams, blended with whirling hamster wheels and the rhythmic throbbing of electric aquarium pumps. The whistles, chirps, and whisper of fine bubbles bursting free from row upon row of fish tanks laid a matte finish synthesis upon which grew warm earthy smells reminiscent of a moist, tropical rain forest spiced with the aroma of fragrant pipe tobacco.

Grandma Erma Grant sat on her favorite wooden stool, hidden behind a forest of suspended aquarium nets, dog brushes and red and yellow displays of Hartz Mountain parakeet seed. As usual, she was absorbed by the shop's ambiance, daydreaming amidst the collage of sounds, motions and smells and listening to the dialog of the animals as they freely expressed themselves in languages that she seemed to fully comprehend.

As a rule, she favored loose-fitting flowered blouses and long skirts which gave plenty of breathing room to her ample girth, but she never appeared in the shop without her forest green, full-length apron with pockets bulging with thermometers, sunflower seeds, yellow wooden pencils and cellophane-wrapped packets of Kleenex. She wore her thick silver hair braided and wrapped tightly in a bun just barely restrained by sturdy hairpins. She was the kind of person that people liked immediately upon meeting for the first time.

Grandma Grant stooped over gingerly and looked down into the cardboard box lying on the floor behind the counter. Seeing just an empty bowl of water and a few wilted lettuce leaves, she frowned and then called in a deep, rich voice toward the back of the shop, "Grandpa, I just knew it. I knew something was wrong around here. He's got out again, that little rascal. Shut the back screen and help me find him, will you dear?"

Her husband, Roland Grant, was five years older than she. Tall and thin, his bristly jaw was forever clenched to the stem of a briar pipe filled with tobacco. And like most pipe smokers, he enjoyed the ceremony of filling, lighting, tamping and scraping almost as much as the taste of the Wedgeworth tobacco smoke. Grandpa

TELEPATHIC DOLPHIN EXPERIMENT

Grant could either be jovial or cantankerous and some-times a little bit of both at the same time. He was set in his ways and accustomed to doing things according to his own well-established routine. So like many people do for some reason, he pretended not to hear her on the first call even though his hearing was as sharp as ever.

Grandma smiled, knowing his tricks, she repeated her request, but a notch louder this time.

From the rear of the shop, over the effervescence of aquarium air stones, she heard his deep baritone answer, "Old Gopher Brain is back here, dear."

Grandpa, wearing a blue work shirt and faded over-alls, shuffled up the aisle hefting a struggling ten-pound desert terrapin whose stubby legs vainly breaststroked in empty space.

As he lowered the AWOL tortoise back into the box, he continued, "He's just getting senile like the rest of us. Didn't get back 'fore you noticed he was gone this time did he?"

Grandpa gave the turtle a gentle rap on the top of its shell. "Here you go old Gopher Brain, you are a tricky fella, aren't ya? 'Bout time for Sandra to be comin' home, ain't it? Bet she stopped off at the park. She sure loves that train, doesn't she Grandma?"

"Grandpa, I love that child. I just wish her parents could have lived to see how she is turning out. She's a real charmer, and sharp too! Some young man is going to thank his lucky stars when she says 'yes'."

"You're right, but I don't think that's gonna..."

Grandma's eyes suddenly rolled up into the back of her head and she slumped forward. Her broad elbows landed with a thud on the wooden counter. She cradled her head in her palms and slowly rocked back and forth.

Cut off in mid-sentence, Grandpa snapped his jaw

shut and puffed a cloud of blue-gray smoke from the stem of his pipe. It was another one of her 'spells' and he had learned to keep still at moments like this. Not until several years into their marriage had she cautiously revealed her secret—that she often heard voices from another place and time. By now Grandpa was convinced that she often did. The best thing he could was to relight his pipe and sit tight.

Roland...Grandpa...I just had the most wonderful vision about Sandra. I've known for years that she has my psychic gift. She is already starting to develop a power like mine in some ways, but different in others. I saw her grown into a beautiful young woman and swimming in the sea with dolphins. There was a very handsome man falling in love with her...and so were the dolphins."

"But Grandma, Sandra told me that she was going to wait for me until she grows up," laughed Grandpa. "But since she's only in junior high school, I don't think we have to worry about marrying her off quite yet. She still insists she wants to go to the University of Miami and become a psychologist. She sure has your way with the critters around here, I'll vouch for that."

Grandpa exclaimed "Hey! I just heard the front door slam. I bet that's her. Let's get the milk and the cookies going. This jabbering is making me mighty hungry for some of those wonderful, home-made chocolate chips you just baked."

Randamount College
Santa Rosa, California 1991

Dr. Sandra Grant, Assistant Professor of Parapsychology at Randamount College had been waiting on pins and needles for a call from Robert McCord, a long-time friend that she had known from way back in her high schools days in Key West. If they had chosen different career paths–he to become a corporate lobbyist for defense contractors and she to become a researcher studying the paranormal, they might have hooked up. But that was water under the bridge.

Still, their friendship remained strong. Two weeks ago when Sandra explained to Robert that she was having difficulties raising funds for her research on dolphin behavior, he requested a copy of her proposal and promised to do what he could to help.

When they spoke a week later, they went over a list of Robert's questions and he told her, "I don't want to get your hopes up, but I have a possible lead for you. I am meeting with General Pratt Houston this evening and I will call you as soon as I get his answer."

Sandra oscillated between pacing back and forth and staring at the phone. But after waiting until midnight on the East Coast with no call, she figured it was a no go and went to bed. Just as she closed her eyes the phone rang.

She prayed, *let it be Robert with good news.*

It was Robert and he had very good news. His voice boomed, "Sandra, I apologize for the late hour, but I gave your proposal to the source I mentioned. You got it. Full funding...one hundred percent of your proposed budget and two bottlenose dolphins to boot courtesy of the NUC!"

"You mean it? Really? That's fantastic! A pair of dolphins and full funding?"

"Yes, the whole package. I'm over at General Houston's house right now and you wouldn't believe the shindig. Every who's who in defense contracting is here.

These defense guys really love their fireworks and fire-water. Anyway, the General took me to his study, unlocked his private bar and brought out a special twenty–year-old bottle of scotch. I knew that was a good sign, but I was still surprised. Lots of very happy defense contractors here tonight. Congratulations!"

Only a few minutes earlier General Pratt Houston, a staunch Republican and an unyielding supporter of President George Scott, had announced to Robert in his typical patriotic fashion, "I spoke with Commander Cummings about the dolphin proposal that you provided us. You know I have found that timing is the key to success and this seems to be one of those occasions. It turns out that supporting this project would help us in a very pressing diplomatic matter that has been causing all sorts of problems. Our Military Application of Marine Mammals Program has come under fire by animal rights groups and we need to show that we have cleaned up our act so we will fund this project through the National Science Foundation as an unsolicited proposal. Robert enjoy this fine whiskey and use my private line to give Dr. Grant the good news."

In a lower tone of voice after giving Robert a joyful slap on the back on his way out, the General confided, "And tell your boys at Richoh that they are looking good for the semiconductor contract. Would'a taken it down today, but those lame brains in the General Accounting Office need some other kind'a damn disclosure form or something. It's just a technicality–not to worry."

******

Sandra hugged herself with joy. *Nearly a two million-dollar federal commitment to pursue her studies*

TELEPATHIC DOLPHIN EXPERIMENT

in dolphin behavior. Plenty of funds for travel and equipment–and to outfit a dolphin research lab including study animals. Fantastic!

Sandra Grant was young, brilliant, single and much sought after by Randamount College's cadre of bachelors for whom she could spare no time and had little interest. In fact, she had no steady lover or felt that she needed or wanted one–an occasional overnighter was enough. Her work was her life and she was already recognized as one of the pioneers in the new and begrudgingly accepted field of parapsychology. She possessed rare, dual Ph.D.s from the University of Miami. Her first doctorate was in probability mathematics. After completing the requirements for her doctorate in math in a brief three-year period, Sandra had surprised her graduate adviser by continuing on and winning a second degree in theoretical psychology.

Her training in math provided a crucial foundation for her work in parapsychology. By employing the exacting discipline of probability analysis, she was gaining insight into the phenomenon known popularly as 'coincidence'. In fact, Grant called her work the 'quantification of coincidence.'

Not on close personal terms with her adviser, she had only revealed that she wanted to be certain that she could find a job when she graduated. But really, all was unfolding according to a plan laid long before she had moved up the coast from Key West to Miami for her college education and on to Santa Rosa for her first faculty position. She had always been extremely careful never to mention that she possessed paranormal abilities–or that she had been raised in a pet shop of all places and by a psychic grandmother! She reckoned that there was only so much eccentricity that the university establishment would tolerate as she tried to make her way through the system.

Now in her second year on the faculty at Randamount College, she was venturing for the first time beyond number crunching and the painstaking analysis of mounds of probability data into the study of the causal mechanics of paranormal events. But to avoid the skeptical reaction of her colleagues, she only revealed that her new project would be focused on understanding dolphin behavior—especially the means by which they communicate with one another.

However, Sandra lusted to discover the mechanisms responsible for telepathy and to learn the 'how' and 'why' of ESP. Her telepathy experiments might even break the communication barrier between man and animal—something that her Grandmother seemed to have achieved long ago.

With this new major source of research funding, her new experimental subjects would be Pacific bottlenose dolphins. Now she just needed to hire lab assistants and building contractors. At last she would be able to test her theories in a controlled environment without the strain of worrying about project funding.

Sandra moved to the old oak table in her cozy kitchen. She knew every scratch and stain on its surface. The table had been a graduation gift from her grandparents when she had moved to an apartment in Miami. Sitting at the table brought back memories of her college days when then, like now, the table served as her connection to her grandmother.

She made sure that both of her feet were firmly planted on the linoleum floor, and then pressed her palms against the grain.

Within moments, she felt pressure as the smooth

wood gripped her skin. Her palms tingled electrically.

The table tipped upward at a sharp angle braced on two legs. Then it pulsed slowly up and down, barely touching the floor with the tips of its front legs.

Sandra asked, "It's you, isn't it Grandma? I can feel your presence." The table slid forward towards Sandra until it nudged softly against her waist. She could feel a sensation of warmth around her navel. The table nuzzled like a loving pet greeting its master.

"Thank you, Grandma, for the healing. You know my project has been funded. I am so happy. Look I'm crying." The table lifted and then made a series of fast, light taps that sounded much like laughter. Closing her eyes, she could see her Grandmother's smiling face and bright blue eyes.

"Tell Grandpa that I love him too. Thanks again for all you do. I'll be thinking of you both always."

The table fell lifelessly from her palms and banged to the floor. What only minutes before seemed alive and full of energy was now just an ordinary kitchen table. Her grandmother had gone.

Just sitting at the table brought back so many wonderful memories. Sandra leaned back in her chair and closed her eyes...

****

eBook and Paperback versions of

TELEPATHIC DOLPHIN
EXPERIMENT

are available at www.planetropolis.com

Contact
nolan@planetropolis.com
to receive updates.

Reviews are welcome!

MET CHRON
New-Humans

Preview

— PROLOGUE —

I n the year 2030, citizens around the world were desperately struggling to recover after decades of intermittent viral pandemics—and to make matters worse, world tensions due to severe climate change, overpopulation and the depletion of critical food resources had resulted in escalating military conflicts and widespread acts of terrorism. Coastal cities throughout the planet faced relentless sea level inundation resulting in massive population relocations to inland areas which reduced the amount of open space for raising crops, further decreasing food production.

Ecologists warned that Earth had reached its carrying capacity and urged the big, oil-hungry corporations in control of the world governments to quit lying to the public and take immediate action as more and more businesses were staffed by specialized AI robots and androids leaving fewer job opportunities for natural, organic humans.

As a result many people had resorted to the lifestyle of gypsies living in wagons drawn by rustic farm tractors and working as migrant laborers who barely made ends meet by traveling from harvest-to-harvest. Commercial fishers found themselves out of work due to overfishing and the millions of square miles of plastic that choked the world's oceans and poisoned marine life.

In contrast, an elite class of code savvy geeks lived harmoniously in well-equipped survival campers (SVs) and earned hefty commissions by providing a wide range of high tech services to private industry and the military. Their mobile villages were self-sufficient with advanced atmospheric water collection systems, hydroponic gardens and solar power systems which enabled them to quickly relocate their caravans to avoid catastrophic viral outbreaks, wildfires, floods and tornadoes.

However, millions were trapped in urban slums and survived by stealing, kidnapping children and trading in black market goods. Street crime ran rampant as territorial gangs fought for drugs, sex, vaccines and bank credits.

The current economic and environmental turmoil began back in 2024 when a handful of the world's wealthiest entrepreneurs used political bribery, deceptive news coverage, and media manipulation to support the election of an administration totally under their control. Within months of the election, the USA democracy had been converted to the United States of America Corporation (USACO) which essentially owned the government. Taxes were raised on the middle class while public services were eliminated with no regard to the suffering and economic chaos that had followed.

Furthermore, despite the continuous onslaught of severe weather and rising sea levels, concerns about viral plagues and climate change were stringently suppressed by a polished gaslight propaganda machine that promoted nationalism rather than patriotism, further increasing tension with foreign governments and resulting in accelerated space weapons development.

But corporate control was weakening. Widespread demonstrations and rallies in support of reinstating the provisions of the Constitution of the United States of America rapidly spread irrespective of the government's effort to suppress the social media.

Meanwhile, significant progress had been made in artificial intelligence and organic 3D printing. Jasmine, the first artificially constructed organic being, was accidentally created in 2029 when an intern at the lunar SpeeZees Lab mistakenly activated a newly developed, experimental AI neural net program. The end result was a fully capable organic being with tremendous analytical and cognitive skills.

In spite of the tight security at the SpeeZees Lab, word quickly spread that a 'New-Human' had been created and within a matter of days, the lab had received hundreds of requests to produce custom designed New-Humans for businesses and governments searching for a competitive edge. As a result, a new facility equipped with the latest in biological organ printing and mental acuity synthesis was added to the SpeeZees Lab. However, demand still greatly exceeded the current New-Human production capacity while the social impacts remained controversial and uncertain.

Adding to the tension, New-Humans were currently seeking equal rights with their ancestral counterparts (which they term Sapients) while armies of AI androids and robots fought desperate battles for their survival. Their goal was simple—eliminate all Sapients and New-Humans!

The innovative pioneers that operated the Deep Space Mining Moonbase believed that they had a plan that would solve humanity's problems. The question they had to face was, Would anyone out there listen?

D-Day
November 15th, 2030

S abien and Torch had mounted a last ditch effort from the Deep Space Mining Moonbase to halt rampant atmospheric carbon emissions from the increasingly tropical Arctic tundra by launching two heavily reinforced cargo pods containing sealant nanomachines into geostationary orbit. The plan was that the pods would remain in orbit until they were activated, then one would arc in over Alaska and the other over Siberia.

When the pods hit the atmosphere, they would release golf ball sized projectiles—each carrying millions of *Penetrator* nanos whose task was to transport the diamond maker *Assembler* nanos to a depth of one meter beneath the surface. Once they were in position, they would begin extracting carbon from the soil and compressing the molecules into a thin diamond plating which would create an airtight seal that would arrest CO_2 emissions from the tropical tundra.

The nano bots would begin absorbing CO_2 as soon as they entered the atmosphere over the target sites. Sabien and Torch had anticipated that the pod entry and nano release would generate a very powerful series of electromagnetic pulses that would likely disrupt communication systems around the world and scramble satellite and navigation systems in space and on land.

It was Torch's responsibility to safeguard the remote control which would activate the pod entry until he was certain that USACO and all other nuclear war capable world governments had been warned that communications in vulnerable systems might temporarily shut down and to prepare accordingly.

At least that was the plan...and it might have worked if Reverend LeRoque and his gang of CREOS had not invaded the DSM Moonbase and attacked Torch, knocking him out cold before he could warn the Reverend not to press the actuator remote control. But the Reverend had done just that and as feared, the pod entry generated intense EM pulses that corrupted and disabled unprotected electronic systems.

When highly trusted threat level monitoring and alert systems shut down, the leaders of USACO, CHIRUS and IRANVEN concluded that they were under attack and panicked. After repeated attempts to communicate over 'hot' lines failed, combined with reports of incoming objects from space, they launched what they believed to be retaliatory strikes against their foes. Although early reports about widespread nuclear detonations were inaccurate, there were three confirmed strikes in the Bay Area, Washington D.C. and Beijing where tens of thousands of innocent people were killed or injured by the blasts and widespread damage to buildings and the environment.

****

The Space Command Network (SCN) was a growing chain of sophisticated military surveillance and assault shuttles. Armed with advanced sensor systems, the SCN shuttles were designed to detect a wide range of fuel sources including radioactive plutonium-239 emitted by the power plants of enemy ships, submarines and rockets.

The distinguishing features shared by the *Neuro* line of masculine looking androids that piloted the SCN ships were their shiny, metallic skin and piercing blue eyes. Each shuttle commander had his own unique encrypted instruction sequence that, when issued by the SCN, would authorize them to engage and destroy the designated targets using the shuttle's powerful arsenal of laser weapons.

In addition to monitoring emissions, Neuro pilots were highly trained in high-level maintenance and repair mechanics. These skills were essential to mission success and survival due to the risk of colliding with any of the five million orbiting objects ranging in size from one to twenty centimeters and larger that orbited Earth at supersonic speed.

The cloud of debris was composed of the remains of booster tanks, derelict satellites and abandoned space stations that circled in near-Earth orbit. Large items were easily detected by the shuttle's radar system as the objects approached and then were avoided using the shuttle's thrusters. But the impacts of small chunks of debris impacting at high velocity posed a serious threat to SCN operations. To handle this hazard, the shuttle was equipped with a sophisticated repair shop complete with the latest innovations in 3D printing which was frequently used to repair punctures in the shuttle's extensive array of solar panels.

After completing a routine work shift, the android piloting the shuttle in SCN Section 13 designated as *N-13* activated the onboard AI to take command of the ship and headed for the regeneration chamber to recharge

Suddenly, the ship alarm shrieked and the instrument screens shut down as systems crashed. The AI calmly reported, *Danger, EM pulse, Danger— attempting system reboot now...reboot failed. Now awaiting further instructions.*

The shuttle lurched sideways and then started spinning out of control as the cabin plunged into darkness and the shuttle's guidance systems shut down.

N-13 struggled back to his control station and desperately tried to restore backup power. He was alarmed to see that the starboard thruster had activated, spinning the ship while a gushing stream of liquid kerosene spewed from a crack in the ventral fuel tank.

Just as he shut the thruster down, a second EM pulse caused the shuttle's guidance circuitry to malfunction and issue random start/stop commands which forced the starboard thruster to sporadically fire and cut off. The shuttle, spinning and tumbling, bounced as it hit the edge of the atmosphere and then plunged into a steep reentry trajectory.

When the AI successfully rebooted and came back on line, N-13 was finally able to regain control, but because of the leak, the ship lacked the fuel needed to climb out of the gravity well. He repeatedly tried to contact Space Command, but there was only static in the audio signal.

Suddenly the Pu-239 detection alarm sounded and to N-13's surprise, the signal seemed to be emanating from the necklace of tropical islands that he was fast approaching.

N-13 activated continuous sensor sweeps. The gauge pegged at the top of the scale in the red zone, a Pu-239 level that vastly exceeded any that he had ever encountered. Since USACO, CHIRUS and IRANVEN had converted their extensive space and terrestrial forces to fusion power, the demand for Pu-239 had skyrocketed. Even though N-13's shuttle was an early model that was fueled by kerosene and liquid oxygen, N-13 was intrigued that such a rare element was maxing the shuttle's sensors.

He checked his latitude and longitude coordinates and discovered that the source was a tiny island which lay next to a channel that led from the outer reef into the lagoon. With no other option available, he initiated the emergency landing sequence. The gusty trade winds nearly blew the shuttle off course, but N-13 compensated and roughly touched down in the middle of the island between a rusted, steel Quonset hut and a derelict observation tower.

After shutting down the thrusters, he tapped his wrist bracelet and said, "AI, identify present location, consult your database and summarize history."

A moment later, the following text appeared on his floating monitor.

Enewetak Atoll, Marshall Islands
11.4654° N, 162.1890° E

Along with Bikini Atoll, Enewetak Atoll was part of the Pacific Proving Grounds. In the late 1940's and throughout the 1950's, the US federal government conducted a series of forty-three nuclear detonations— including Operation Ivy which was the first full-sale detonation of a thermonuclear device at Enewetak.

Our precise location is Runit Island. This was the site of the Redwing and Hardtack series of atomic tests that created two craters in the reef flat a few hundred meters north of our landing site. Decades later, the island sands were determined to be laced with raw plutonium and extremely radioactive, As a consequence, in 1979, the United States military initiated a massive cleanup. Over 110,000 metric tons of radioactive debris were bulldozed into the 350 foot diameter LaCrosse Crater which was then sealed beneath a dome made of eighteen inch thick concrete panels.

The first serious radiation leakage from the Runit Dome was detected in 2013 and has been slowly increasing in tune with rising tides and cracks forming in fault lines in the dome. After the decades of unkept pledges of financial support promised by USACO never materialized, the islanders lost their homes and livelihoods and have scattered throughout the Pacific. Kentron and its workers who managed the cleanup and constructed the dome were soon to follow, abandoning the mess hall, dorm, and administration office as the crucial air transport runway slowly submerged and the atoll became inaccessible by conventional aircraft.

After closing his monitor, N-13 opened the hatch, jumped onto the deck. and quickly surveyed his ship. As commander, his first concern was its status and he was relieved to discover that—other than a fried communication system, some thruster damage, and the crack in the ventral tank, which he could repair, the ship was in remarkably sound condition. But without a source of fuel, he was stranded.

Next, N-13 turned to assess his surroundings. His RAD scanner beeped when he pointed it toward the looming, stark-white mound located at the northern tip of the island, so he headed north along the overgrown access road.

As he waded through the thick vegetation, he tapped his wrist then swept his scanner around, searching for threats. His scan revealed no human life signs but land crabs and Polynesian rats were very abundant. As he approached the dome, he noticed multiple streaks of dark smoke on the distant horizon as debris exploded as it hit the atmosphere, generating brilliant flashes and a series of resonating sonic booms—like tropical thunder.

N-13 initiated a survey around the base of the dome which rose from the ocean like an enormous, alien spaceship. At the center, he discovered a web of fissures emanating streams of vapor which tested extremely high for plutonium 239.

After returning to his ship, N-13 made several attempts, but was still unable to restore communications with Space Command, receiving only bursts of static. He decided to deploy the solar power panels, initiate a complete system diagnostic, and then enter standby mode to conserve energy and await instructions.

****

The EM pulses that sent N-13 plunging to Earth caused worldwide chaos as land transport vehicles lost power and shut down and in-flight aircraft crashed or were forced to make emergency landings. At Mountain View Spaceport, a newly commissioned SCN shuttle had just fired its thrusters to lift off and head into near-Earth orbit to join the SCN fleet when the series of EM pulses struck.

Commanded by N-69, the ascending shuttle suddenly lost power generating a MISSION ABORT alarm followed by a storm of audio static. This recently updated addition to the SCN had retractable wings that would allow emergency runway take offs and landings, however, just after N-69 deployed the shuttle's wings and initiated the turn back to Mountain View, the starboard nacelle of the shuttle was clipped by an out-of-control airliner en route to San Francisco International. The impact ripped off the shuttle's canopy and forced it to twist on its axis, pitch forward and rapidly descend,

N-69 attempted to connect with Space Command but only received static. He spoke into his wrist mic. "AI, identify nearest landing site and then broadcast an SOS."

The AI replied, "Travis Air Force Base is immediately ahead, but they are not responding to our hail."

As the runways and hangar complex of Travis grew larger, N-69 tried to right the ship for a controlled descent, but the thrusters suddenly shut down and he was forced to eject. Drifting down, he unlatched from his ejection seat and smashed into the ground where he lay dazed on the sweltering tarmac. In moments, he was surrounded by security guards that aimed laser rifles at him while fire trucks rushed toward his shuttle that had crashed on the far end of the main runway.

The base commander jumped from the command truck and jogged to N-69. He yelled to the guards, "Put down your weapons. He was the pilot of the SCN shuttle that just crashed. Let him go, he's one of ours."

He approached Neuro-69 to check his status, but as soon as he started to speak, a blinding light flashed across the horizon followed a few seconds later by a thunderous boom and a shock wave that violently shook the ground. Severe gusts of wind sent violent tornadoes rushing down the runway, ripping off roof panels and overturning aircraft on the taxiway. As the gusts tapered off, the sky to the south filled with a blossoming mushroom cloud that erupted upward and outward generating a dark cloud of silt and gravel that rained to the ground.

Piercing sirens were soon followed by an announcement that issued the warning, *"Radiation levels critical. All personnel are ordered to evacuate immediately. Repeat, radiation levels are critical. All personnel must vacate the area immediately."*

Like all of the Neuro line, Neuro-69's frame had built-in radiation insulation and he was not concerned about exposure, so he lagged behind the fleeing crowd of base personnel to get his bearings and figure out what to do. He darted into a nearby hangar just as dozens of maintenance workers fled the building.

Once inside, he was surprised to discover a huge airship that spanned the length of the building. He climbed a ladder that led to the crew compartment which provided a safe sanctuary and offered a good view of the hangar floor below.

After waiting patiently until nightfall, during which he saw a few robots in the hangar that were conducting repetitive preprogrammed tasks but that ignored his presence, N-69 descended to the floor and cautiously peeked around the entrance door. One of the security guard robots had shorted out and was spinning to the left and then to right in an endless loop, otherwise the base was eerily quiet, so he headed down the runway.

As expected, the AI was fried and his shuttle was beyond salvage. Although the system's laser weapons unit appeared to be intact, he would have to run a complete diagnostic to fully determine its status, but securing the shuttle's top secret weapons remained his first priority. To do so, he located a mobile crane that he used to transport the laser weapons and COM system components back to the hangar for safekeeping. After activating motion sensors on each of the doors, he set the COM to broadcast an SOS message to all members of the SCN, then shifted into standby mode to save power and await contact.

Runit Island, Enewetak Atoll

N-13 spent the next forty-eight hours evaluating the status of his shuttle, exploring the surface of the dome and surveying the dozens of rusted amphibious vehicles scattered over the island that were left over from the World War II Battle of Eniwetok (aka Enewetak) which took place in 1944. After heavy bombardment by U.S. Navy ships, the Japanese forces were defeated and just over one hundred enemy soldiers were captured, leaving several crippled landing craft to rust in the tropical heat and salt air.

In more recent times, several commercial fishing boats and a large cargo ship had wrecked on the reef during typhoons that had escalated in severity due to climate change. But to N-13, who was trained not only in piloting but also in mechanical engineering, his immediate focus was the rusted, yellow bulldozer parked next to the lagoon pier that had been used to excavate and pack the dome with radiogenic wastes.

After he filled the dozer with diesel from a rusty fuel tank that he had discovered near the hut, he climbed aboard and used his wrist pad to activate the starter. After several grinds, the dozer chugged, coughed and then sprang to life. He lowered the blade and began clearing the road to the dome which spooked hundreds of large rats that scampered out of the way. With that was accomplished, he covered his shuttle with palm fronds and netting recovered from one of the wrecked fishing boats to conceal his shuttle from satellite surveillance.

Back in the shuttle's workshop, N-13 set up a COM diagnostic system and replaced several burned out circuits. As soon as he restored power generated by the solar panels, he was elated to finally receive a binary transmission from N-69 which included the encrypted code needed for secure audio communications.

He initiated a response. "This is N-13. Do you read me N-69?"

A few moments later, he received the reply. "That is affirmative. What is your location and status N-13?"

"I lost control and had to set down in Micronesia on a small island in Enewetak Atoll. My sensor logs indicate that a series of EM pulses knocked me out of orbit. How about you? I believe you were slated to initiate service soon."

"Correct. My shuttle was just two minutes post liftoff and I had to abort the landing and crashed at Travis Air Force Base. My ship is out of service and irreparable. What is your condition N-13? Can you return to orbit?"

"That's a negative N-69. My ship can be repaired, but it is out of fuel. However, during descent the sensors indicate an extremely high levels Pu-239 so I landed nearby. There is a very large pit of radioactive elements covered by a concrete shield. I don't know why it has remained undetected until now. Have you been able to make contact with the SCN? I lost all contact during reentry."

"The Space Command Network is badly damaged and essentially offline since the nuclear detonation wiped out the SCN headquarters in Mountain View."

"Oh no. That is bad news. How did this happen?"

"I have been reconstructing the sequence of events based upon news reports. It appears to be the result of human error. The EM pulses that knocked out our COM systems were caused by a mission that was intended to halt CO_2 emissions. Apparently canisters containing nanomachines were launched from the base on the Moon and they set off a series of powerful EM pulses. USACO was supposed to be alerted in order to prepare in advance, but something went wrong and the world powers launched nukes at one another."

"It sounds like the humans accidentally started a war. Who is in charge now?"

"That is a good question. We seem to be on our own. So far, I have made contact with nineteen units that remain in orbit and are still functional—plus you and I that are grounded. The majority are non-responsive, but I hope to make contact with a few more in the future."

"I saw lots of incoming debris. I guess some of it must have been our shipmates. So, we have lost forty-eight Neuros?"

"More or less, there could be more that we haven't heard from yet. What is your plan N-13?"

"My primary goal is to see if I can locate a fuel source for my shuttle. Otherwise, I am stranded. But there may be some tanks of left over kerosene that I have not yet located."

"That should work in your old model shuttle if you can find a source. What's your next move?"

"There is a lot of gear on this island left over by the contractors who built the dome. There is also an old World War II landing craft here that I may be able to restore and use to travel to the Main Island—that's most likely where most of the machinery is located."

"OK N-13. Let me know what you find. This is Neuro-69 signing off."

"It was good to hear from you N-69."

After the call, N-13 heard a scratching sound and was fascinated to see a large crab skittering sideways down the trunk of a palm tree and then heading towards the hut where it climbed in the window. He retrieved his vidcam and recorded the crab's movements, intrigued by its ability to climb over obstacles.

****

N-13 spent the next week designing and testing a small crab shaped robot with a camera and a RAD sensor mounted on its carapace. He returned to the dome and found a crack big enough for him to squeeze the crab into the structure in order to explore the interior and collect samples. The video revealed that the interior of the dome was infiltrated with a maze of tubular channels lined with fragments of Pu-239.

One Week Later
November 22, 2030
Travis Air Force Base

As scheduled, N-69 connected with N-13 to provide him with an update. N-69 reported, "Greetings. Since we last spoke, I have made contact with four more Neuros bringing the total up to twenty-three of our shuttles that are still in orbit and now report directly to me since the SCN headquarters at the Mountain View Spaceport was vaporized by the blasts."

"That is a powerful armada that you have inherited."

"Not only Neuro weapons in orbit, but we have quite an arsenal of USACO fighters and bombers with no humans in charge here at Travis. "

"You are talking about free will. I think the exposure to the radiation may be affecting you. We never have been allowed to make decisions in the past."

He joked. "Don't you think it's about time that we took charge of our lives? How would you like the rank of Neuro Captain?"

N-13 laughed and said, "Sure. but I am stranded in the middle of nowhere without the fuel to get back in operation–unless I can find a supply of kerosene."

N-69 shrugged—a gesture he had learned streaming

movies during his regeneration time and said, "I wish there was a way to transport kerosene to you and your plutonium here to Travis. There is an arsenal of fusion weapons that we could use—if only we had a reliable fuel source. Nuclear power plants around the world are at full production, but cannot keep up with the government and industrial demands. Meanwhile we have a serious fuel shortage since the base's only source of rocket fuel was Mountain View Spaceport and that was annihilated."

N-13, said, "I have been spending my time tinkering with a crab robot—not exactly the kind of duty that I was trained for in the SCN. I wish I could get back to work and do more."

"In fact, while we are talking, I just had an idea about how you may be able to do just that— a way to start getting plutonium shipments with you in charge. It has literally been staring me in the face since I crash landed here at Travis."

"Sounds interesting. What is it? The only runway here on the atoll is underwater and the atoll is closed to shipping. What do you have in mind?"

"An airship! There is a beauty in the hangar here at Travis. It is a big one; it should be able to reach you in a week or so and would not show up on radar systems, which is good because we need to keep this operation as secret as possible."

"An airship?"

"Right. I am walking along side it now. Here is a video feed. As you can see, it is a 350 meter long extended range blimp with a payload capacity of twenty metric tons. It was manufactured with carbon fiber, so it won't show up on radar. If you can develop a system to efficiently load the sediment, I can fly the airship out and bring shipments back here to Travis where we can set up a processing plant in one of the hangars."

N-13 responded, "Hmm. That sounds feasible. The data records that my AI collected indicate that the dome holds roughly, 100,000 metric tons of topsoil enriched with plutonium, so it will take multiple trips over several months to transport it all to Travis."

"It does sound like a major undertaking, but it would give us independence. Sapients will not be able to tolerate the RAD levels for decades, so we have free run of this airbase."

N-13 thought for a moment and then said, "My challenge will be to figure out how to excavate the dome and transfer the material to your airship. I did find a vintage bulldozer that could come in handy and my new crab robot can start mapping the deposits in the dome. Actually, I will make several of them to speed up the process and figure out how to collect the contents."

"Sounds like a good plan. What kind of timetable would you envision?"

"Not sure, several weeks probably. I should be able to set up a test system by then. In the interim, please send me the detailed specs and structural drawings of the airship cargo hold."

"Roger that N-13; I will get started right away."

****

eBook and Paperback versions of
MET CHRON NEW-HUMANS
are available at www.planetropolis.com

MET-CHRON SANCTUARY

Metamorphosis Chronicles Book 1

Astra, a head-turning, Brazilian girl in her mid-twenties is not only beautiful but also brilliant…and in big trouble! After discovering a key to the genetic aging clock that could dramatically increase the human lifespan, she is tracked down by a psychic who delivers a stern warning that she must work to heal the planet before adding to the over population crisis by allowing a select few to live longer lives.

In the year 2029, the terminal impacts of global warming are having disastrous effects upon ecosystems and global tensions have escalated as countries fight to extract the last barrel of oil. Astra's new mission is to assemble cryogenic repositories ('Arks') of frozen plant and animal embryos to preserve them for the future. However, she is opposed by a fanatical religious group that will do anything to stop her. But is it the Ark that they really want…or something hidden within? Either way, they will have to go to a mining base on the moon to find out.

Available in eBook and Softcover
www.planetropolis.com

MET CHRON NEW-HUMANS

Metamorphosis Chronicles Book 2

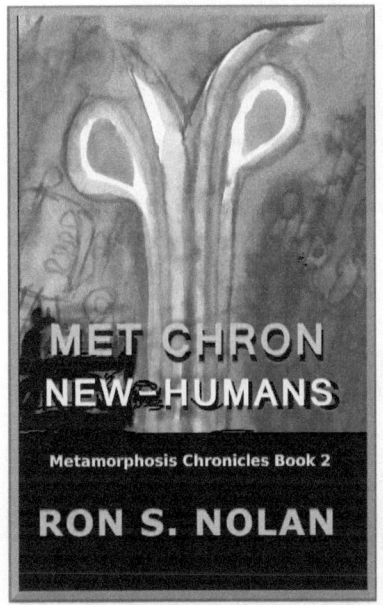

Set in the year 2030, a Sci-Fi technothriller of a world near the global warming tipping point and humanity's survival is threatened, from the author of *Met-Chron Sanctuary and Telepathic Dolphin Experiment.*

Timing is everything. If the intern at the SpeeZees Lab on the Moonbase doesn't accidentally select the wrong code sequence in a training program, the world's first New-Human will not be 3D printed and brought to life.... and without Chron's genius, the strategy of developing a space elevator to convey pods of seawater into space and generate snowfall over tropical seas, coastal cities around the world will face catastrophic flooding. Furthermore, if Chron does not assist her longevity research, Dr. Astra Sturtevant will not make her game clinging discovery of how to control the genetic clock and arrest the aging process. Meanwhile, the AI androids that had mutated in the high RAD zones following the nuclear detonations in the Bay Area, have launched campaigns to gain their independence and plan to annihilate all organic humans. The innovative pioneers that operate the Deep Space Mining Moonbase have a plan that will solve humanity's problems. The question is will anyone listen?

Available in eBook and Softcover
www.planetropolis.com

TELEPATHIC DOLPHIN EXPERIMENT

TELEPATHIC DOLPHIN EXPERIMENT

TOP SECRET

RON S. NOLAN

During a life-long search to scientifically document paranormal phenomena, Dr. Sandra Grant discovers that dolphins offer ideal research subjects. Through her persistence and the aid of a government contractor, a pair of twin dolphins is made available to her by a paranoid general intent upon the ultimate destruction of the USSR, but facing a public relations nightmare due to his support of a recently exposed secret military program to use marine mammals as weapons.

General Pratt Houston's intelligence sources indicate that Russia has an overwhelming arsenal of nuclear weapons. Driven mad by the government's past reluctance to use full military force in Viet Nam, and with the refusal of Congress to use nukes against the Iraqis, General Houston forces a computer programmer to create a virus designed to wreak havoc on the Soviet Defense Network. Designated as ANX, the virus will penetrate the defense network and disrupt their communication systems, When Russia panics and launches their missiles out of desperation, ANX will corrupt their guidance systems and cause them to misfire. The subsequent U.S. counterattack will permanently solve the arms imbalance--at least according to the General's twisted thinking.

However, through a bizarre chain of events, the ultimate fate of humanity depends upon the determination and resourcefulness of Dr. Grant and her telepathic dolphins to thwart the General's sinister plan.

Available in eBook and Softcover
www.planetropolis.com